Just Julian

Just Julian

MARKUS HARWOOD-JONES

JAMES LORIMER & COMPANY LTD., PUBLISHERS
TORONTO

James Lorimer & Company Ltd., Publishers acknowledges funding support
from the Ontario Arts Council (OAC), an agency of the Government of
Ontario. We acknowledge the support of the Canada Council for the Arts,
which last year invested $153 million to bring the arts to Canadians throughout
the country. This project has been made possible in part by the Government of
Canada and with the support of the Ontario Media Development Corporation.

Cover design: Shabnam Safari
Cover image: Shutterstock

Library and Archives Canada Cataloguing in Publication

Star, 1991-, author
    Just Julian / Markus Harwood-Jones.

(Real love)
Issued in print and electronic formats.
ISBN 978-1-4594-1292-7 (softcover).--ISBN 978-1-4594-1293-4 (EPUB)

    I. Title. II. Series: Real love (Series)

PS8637.T3635J87 2018   jC813'.6   C2017-906501-7
                                                C2017-906502-5

Published by: Distributed in Canada by: Distributed in the US by:
James Lorimer &   Formac Lorimer Books   Lerner Publisher Services
Company Ltd., Publishers 5502 Atlantic Street   1251 Washington Ave. N.
117 Peter Street, Suite 304 Halifax, NS, Canada   Minneapolis, MN, USA
Toronto, ON, Canada   B3H 1G4   55401
M5V 0M3   www.lernerbooks.com
www.lorimer.ca

Printed and bound in Canada.
Manufactured by Friesens Corporation in Altona, Manitoba,
Canada in December 2017.
Job # 239688

For you.

01 It's Over

JULIAN'S CHEEK HITS AGAINST PAVEMENT. *He takes a shaky gasp, then pushes himself up and moves forward, quickly as he can. The end of the parking lot is in sight, a sprout of yellow grass marking its edge. An engine revs behind him, but Julian doesn't spare a second to look back. The sound of his own breath drowns out his thoughts. His chest tight, knees pumping, he makes a break for it. A loud honk blares from just behind him. Try as he might, he can't gain any ground. It's like he's running in molasses. His pursuers are getting closer. He can feel them hot on his back.*

A scream made its way up and out of Julian, shaking him awake. The sheets clung to his body, wet with sweat. He reached for the half-empty glass on his bedside table. Gulping down the water, he tried to wash away the nightmare. When the feelings refused to fade, Julian shoved off the bedding and reached for his paints.

On his feet, Julian threw colours across a busy canvas. He arched sharp turns and pulled strokes to form long, bleeding lines. One foot in the past, one in the present, he dipped his brush in crimson. He ran it across the canvas and watched heavy red droplets roll down. He traced all the times he'd been chased home, all the cruel words, all the times he'd cut the pain out from his own skin.

"It's over, it's over, it's over," he muttered, but the words were hollow. Those years of bullying would never be over. They crept into his nightmares nearly every night. Julian's head was throbbing as he reached for another colour. Memory after memory raked across his mind.

Darkness envelops him. Or it would, if not for the pulsing orange light from the street outside. In the endless twilight, Julian loses track of hours, even days, as he rolls back and forth in bed. Crumpled up, half-written letters to his cousin lie around his mattress beside empty canvases and unopened tubes of paint. His phone, annoying him with its buzzing, is left unanswered. Julian's mother comes with food and kind words, but all Julian sees on her face is pity and resentment.

Julian groaned and clutched his stomach as the guilt turned in his gut. Slapping a hand across his own cheek, he tried to break the cycle of those awful memories. He needed to come back to the present. He'd spent too long cooped up inside, unable to do much else but survive through the worst of his depression. Going over it again and again like this wasn't helping.

"It's over, it's over, it's over," he repeated. He doubted the words even as he said them. Yeah, maybe he had managed to get outside again, even enroll in online courses so he could finish high school. But he couldn't shake the feeling that he was just one small slip away from falling back into the deep pit.

He dipped a wet brush in the dark blue paint, letting it slide across the canvas at an angle. The half-hearted waterfall swirled against the red, turning into whirlpools. Images flashed in Julian's mind like lightning, followed by the thunderclaps of the brush hitting against the canvas. A vision of his mother's brow furrowed in disappointment. His cousin waiting for someone to arrive during visiting hours. His friends wondering why he never returned their calls. Julian pushed them all away with the brush. Pulling pillars of white across the canvas, watching them turn grey, he painted his emptiness. His isolation. His failure.

Julian's stomach tightens as he reads the email over again. A failing grade. One comment, from the faceless online instructor: "Continues to deviate from assignment guidelines." A rush of anger pinches Julian's nose, making his eyes water. He slams the laptop shut, nearly throwing it against the ground. He catches himself — there was no way he or his mom could afford a new one. Instead Julian just scratches his fingernails against his skin, leaving deep, swelling lines along his forearm. This is useless. He is useless. Maybe he's just not meant to finish school. Maybe he's not meant to be alive at all. Maybe everyone would be better off if he just disappeared.

Julian slammed the brush into a dollop of yellow, streaking lines like fire across the painting. His stomach was so tight he was starting to feel sick, but he couldn't stop now. He had to finish. He took the brush in his fingers and ran a fingernail along the edge, splattering black across the canvas. He let himself fall into those black holes amidst the chaos of colour. Their cool invitation reminded him of how comforting it would be to curl back up in bed, to cocoon again.

With a sigh, Julian stepped back. He put the brush behind his ear and took in the artwork. The colours on the canvas bled into one another, a mess in all directions. The brushstrokes told a story of his fears and failures — a rainbow of regret. Hands shaking,

Julian reached for another sip of water. He spit it out, feeling bits of acrylic on his tongue, realizing he had mistakenly grabbed the water for his paints. Much of the mess sprayed onto his hands. Wiping his lips, Julian was struck with a spark of inspiration and went for the brush again.

He traced the brush against his hand, up his arm. The muddy water mapped across the veins running along his wrists and back down to the tips of his fingers. The copper tone was sweet on his skin. He pushed his hand onto the canvas, leaving his mark on the piece. Stepping back, he took a moment to admire the small handprint among the mess of colour and memory.

Julian managed to make his way to the bathroom. He ran warm water over his skin. As he washed away the acrylic flecks, he glanced up and caught his image in the mirror. Julian studied the traces of his mother along the edges of eyes, the dimples in his cheeks, the curve of his round, broad face. But there was something else to the reflection, something he couldn't name, that marked him as the son of a father he could barely remember. Julian tried to peer through the layers, hoping he might find something that was just *him*. With a sigh, he gave up and went back to bed. "It's over, it's over, it's over," he whispered, trying to mean it this time.

02 Collision

JULIAN MINDLESSLY UNPACKED chips and dips into rainbow-themed plastic bowls. Lyla and her girlfriend, Rose, puttered around their new apartment. The couple whispered to each other and broke into a fit of giggles. Julian raised an eyebrow.

Lyla had pleaded with Julian to come over to meet her new girlfriend, to try to have fun for once. That was classic Lyla. When they were nine, she'd convinced Julian they should ride their bikes down the biggest hill she could find, just so they would crash together. At twelve, she got him to skip school with her to get slushies, so they would be caught and get detention together. When they were fourteen, she got him to sneak into an R-rated horror movie, so she'd have someone to scream with — and, of course, so they could get kicked out of the theatre together. So now, at nineteen, here they were again. This time it was her first apartment with her first real girlfriend. It was no surprise she wanted Julian there so, whatever disaster might happen, they would face it together. But this time, Julian was an afterthought.

He heard the couple break into laughter again. Irritation bubbled under his skin. Lyla had moved on and found someone else to drag along on her next big adventure. Julian sighed, mumbling to himself, "Well, it's not her fault her bestie turned out to be a big loser." He went back to arranging the snack table.

Out of tasks to keep himself busy, Julian carved out a spot for himself on the couch. He nervously picked at his nails as the party guests began to arrive. Lyla and her girlfriend, even when surrounded by people, managed a we're-a-couple-look-how-close-we-are look. Julian scowled at his raw cuticles.

Soon the reek of cigarettes, weed, and alcohol began to fill the place. Julian's head started to pound. Parties got boring fast when you were the only one sober. Everything was too damn loud. There were so many people shouting at each other just to be heard, a few singing loudly along with the blaring music. Julian wasn't sure what would be worse — going through the entire party scarcely speaking to another soul, or being forced to make small talk because someone tried to strike up a conversation. As it was, he planned to sit and brood silently on the couch. He would watch people laugh too loud, spill their drinks, and dry-hump on the makeshift living-room dance floor.

Just as Julian had resigned not to move from his spot, Paris made her entrance, all big smiles. Julian squinted as if he'd stepped into a ray of direct sunlight — and was allergic to it. There was no doubt Paris would spot him there, sitting alone on the couch, but he still had a moment as Ms. Popular greeted her unending string of friends throughout the room. While Paris posed for selfies, Julian's anxiety sent him off the couch and deeper into the apartment, looking for a place to hide out.

Julian made it to the bathroom and finally had a chance to take a breath — even if that breath wasn't the most refreshing. With a sigh, he leaned against the wall. He was so over this party. Then there came yelling from the next room, followed by a few loud thumps. "I don't even want to know," Julian murmured to himself. Unfortunately, someone started pounding on the door. "Just a minute!" Julian called, running the tap. He splashed a little water on his face, took a deep breath, and went back out.

Paris bounded over right away. Julian reeled back at first. He prepared himself for her exhaustingly perky disposition. But as she approached, he could see that something was wrong. Her eyes were red and welling up with tears. As Paris reached Julian, he took her arm and pulled her into the bedroom, hoping for a little privacy so she could have a proper breakdown.

The room was a scatter of unpacked boxes and shelves full of books around a plain mattress. Paris sat on the bed and pulled Julian down with her. Tears smeared black eyeliner down her honey-pink cheeks. "He . . . I thought he liked me! So, I . . . Isn't this supposed to be a queer party?! And then he goes and . . . he blasts it to the room that the chick he was talking to — he called me a *man*." Paris buried her face in her hands. "Why would he even?! God, I just hate cis guys!" She let out a muffled scream before adding softly, "No offence."

Julian nodded with understanding. Even though he was cisgender, not transgender like Paris, he'd seen too many friends go through the same kind of thing. He squeezed her arm and leaned forward. At that same moment, Paris looked up and over at him. The two collided — lips first.

The kiss only lasted a moment. Julian pulled back. Paris leaned in again, eyes closed. A pang of guilt hit Julian's chest. He became extremely aware of his body. He was still hugging her. Should he let go? When was a good moment to try to back away? Was there any way now to comfort her without her taking it the wrong way? He froze, running through his options. "This is why I don't talk to people," Julian whispered to himself.

"What?" Paris asked, opening her eyes and pulling back a little.

"Oh! Uh, nothing!" Julian replied.

Paris looked down. Her eyes were still red and puffy. She asked, "Julian, do you like me?"

"Well," Julian began. He started biting his fingernails. "I mean, you're really great."

Paris looked up with a sparkle of hope in her eye. "I've always liked you," she confessed. She took his hands with her own.

"Wow, really," Julian replied. He tried to sound surprised. "I like you too, Paris. But, uh, I just don't know if I like you that way, you know? It's just — I . . ." The room was starting to feel just like the rest of the party — crowded, loud, overwhelming. He couldn't seem to catch his breath. He had to end this somehow. "I'm just going through a lot right now," he concluded.

"Yeah, okay." Paris nodded.

Julian let out a sigh of relief.

"So maybe just one date?" Paris asked, gently biting her lip.

Julian inhaled sharply. Paris had been through so much tonight, he wanted to do the right thing. And it wasn't like he was seeing anyone. He didn't even like anyone. It was just one date . . . What was the worst that could happen? "I guess. I mean, sure," Julian replied, trying to smile.

Paris's face brightened, her smile glimmering like a ray of sunshine coming out from behind a raincloud.

"How about next Friday?" Julian suggested.

Paris's smile spilled out over her cheeks into her dimples. "Friday it is," she replied. She kissed him on the cheek and jumped up. As she opened the bedroom door to return to the party, she didn't seem to notice that Julian stayed behind.

Putting his head in his hands, Julian groaned. "Goddess, what else could possibly go wrong tonight?"

03 *Spark*

THE DOOR OPENED AND CLOSED again with a click. Julian didn't even bother to look up. But then he realized the footsteps making their way into the room definitely did not sound like Paris's heels.

Julian took his face out of his hands and raised his head. He couldn't believe what he was seeing. It looked like an underwear model had found his way out of a magazine fully clothed and parked himself in the middle of Lyla's bedroom. The stranger was tall, athletic, with sweet, pouty lips, and a mess of dark brown hair. The nervous look on his face made Julian wonder if he could be running away from the party too.

Julian looked the handsome stranger over and noticed charming little bits of imperfection — a slanted nose, a scar across his hand, warm, rosy cheeks that were quickly turning bright pink. Julian raised an eyebrow. Normally, it would have bothered Julian to have someone invade his hiding place. He was surprised to find that he welcomed the company of this mysterious and handsome young man.

After a moment, Julian broke the silence. "Hi."

The stranger stayed silent, so Julian took in his outfit — an oversized athletic jacket, bearing the image of a basketball on fire with some team name of which Julian had never heard. With saggy jeans and brand-name, slip-on sneakers, he stood out at a party full of hard-femmes and androgynous punks. This guy looked like the type Julian had learned to avoid. But something about him was different.

The stranger cautiously glanced around the room, clearly making eyes at Julian. Fiddling with a golden ring on his right hand, he looked like he had something to say but couldn't seem to get words out. Julian stood to make the first move.

It had been so long since Julian felt a spark of attraction. Like a moth to the flame, he pulled closer. His heart was beating faster with every step. Julian tried to go slowly, savouring the moment. This guy looked like he might spook easily. Reaching out a hand, Julian brushed his fingers lightly along the young man's cheekbones. He smirked as a shiver visibly ran through the stranger.

That seemed to be enough to get him talking. Finally, he breathed an introduction. "I'm Romeo."

What kind of a name was Romeo? Julian suppressed a laugh.

"Um, I mean, nobody really calls me that. Except my mom, I guess," Romeo started to stammer. "Rome — it's just Rome. I mean, it's actually Romeo Montague. Pretty much everyone just calls me Rome. But you could call me Romeo I guess, if you wanted to . . ."

"Romeo," Julian said. He tested out the name in his mouth. He liked it.

Romeo turned a deeper shade of red. He gulped and nodded. Clearly, he'd run out of words again.

Julian moved forward, gently pushing his fingers into Romeo's thick hair. No more words were needed. Romeo wrapped Julian in an embrace and the two connected. A spark ran through Julian's body. He shivered with delight.

The kiss was imperfect and incredible. Romeo was nervous, pulling back one second and then pushing deeper the next. Julian was rusty, forgetting what to do with his hands or if he was allowed to let out a moan. But, instead of embarrassment, Julian was elated. He never wanted this feeling to end.

Suddenly, the bedroom door came swinging open. The two boys were shoved onto the floor. Julian went first and smacked his head against the ground. He could feel Romeo's weight fall on top of him. Dazed,

Julian looked up at the doorway. He saw a familiar face — one that made his stomach clench with guilt.

Ty stood, arms crossed, scowling down. His face looked strange — brows creased, mouth like a straight line. In Julian's memories, his cousin was always laughing, sappy and sweet, full of funny stories. Now he looked cold and stony. After a moment, Julian realized his cousin's gaze was fixed on the stranger Julian had just been kissing.

Romeo rolled off Julian and jumped up. Ty said something to Romeo in a gruff tone. Julian couldn't make out the words. Behind Ty, Julian saw a small crowd had gathered around the door to peer inside. It was like the whole party had decided to intrude on Romeo and Julian's intimate moment.

Romeo gave Julian a quick glance. Then, just like that, he was gone.

"You okay?" Ty asked Julian, his voice now gentle. He offered Julian a hand to get up. The crowd murmured with excitement at the drama. They leaned in to see what Julian might say. Not interested in feeding their curiosity, Julian got up by himself. He pushed past the group and out of the room.

"Jules, wait!" Ty called after him. "It's not what you think! I know that guy! He's a 'phobe. His buddies were the ones harassing Paris!"

Julian didn't want to turn back — not now. How long had it been since he'd seen his cousin? And this was their reconnection? Julian shook his head. He glanced around one more time for Lyla, but she was nowhere in sight, yet again. With a sigh, he made his way to the door. He was so done with this party.

That night, for the first time in a long time, Julian didn't have nightmares. It might have been because he barely slept. Instead he worked on painting after painting. Trying to remember the feeling of that kiss, he pulled out gentle pinks, sparkling silvers, and deep reds. He traced plump and delicate lines like those of Romeo's lips. He spent half the night experimenting with colours, moving from broad brush strokes to dots of light and shadow. Still he couldn't quite capture how it had felt. The memory was in his body, but it would not allow itself to be moved onto the canvas. Finally, as the early morning light began to break through the window, Julian let himself fall onto the bed. He slipped into fantasies of strong arms pulling him close again. He murmured to himself, "Oh, Romeo . . ."

04 Osborne Afternoon

"SO, HAVE YOU EVER SEEN him around before?"

"Never," Julian sighed. "I'd remember him."

Julian's friend Sami was leading him along familiar storefronts. The sidewalk was peppered with cigarette butts and the windows with rainbow flags. Sami mused, "A strange boy, an epic kiss, a midnight getaway! It's all something out of a queer Cinderella!" Julian's friend spun around, as if a fairy godmother was making a ball gown out of their overalls. "And he didn't even leave a glass slipper," Sami laughed.

"Or, like, a phone number," Julian sighed.

"Ah, well," Sami said to Julian. "A straight-acting jock like that? Running with those guys who messed with Paris? If he even is one of us, he's probably still swimming in confusion and bullshit. Like, the type to tell you that bisexuals have to 'pick a side.' Or argue that using 'they' and 'them' pronouns for someone like me is 'too hard'!" Sami spoke lightly. But there was a cutting tone hiding behind their smile. "Seems to me like you dodged a bullet."

Julian sighed. Sami was probably right. Chewing on his thumbnail, Julian wondered aloud, "Why would a guy like that even be there? Do you think he was trying to crash the party?"

"Maybe he's one of those *no-homo homos*?" Sami spoke in a mock-masculine voice, "Keeping it *on the down-low*?"

Julian just shrugged.

"What do you think?" Sami continued. "Is he the type to have a profile on a hook-up app? Maybe just a picture of his abs and a description that just says, like, *masc 4 masc.*"

Sami grinned but, seeing that Julian wasn't laughing, they quickly changed the subject. Taking Julian by the arm, Sami led him to the benches outside the liquor store where they could people-watch all those wandering by River and Osborne that afternoon. Julian tried to play along. At the very least, the strangers they surveyed might make for good artistic inspiration. There were fluorescent-haired punks pushing a baby carriage. A gaggle of older gals giggled as they made their way to the supermarket. A couple nervous-looking teenagers pushed one another toward the local sex shop, watched by a pair of queens sharing smokes outside the martini bar across the street.

While the sights were entertaining, Julian couldn't help but hope Romeo might make an appearance. He sighed. If Lyla was there, she'd know what to say. She'd be patient and comforting. And she'd manage to snap him out of his love-drunk funk. Sami, on the other hand, seemed to enjoy the drama of it all, and all they did was turn everything into a big joke!

Sami wiggled their eyebrows at him, trying to get his attention. "Who's *really* called Romeo these days anyways?" they scoffed. "Like, okay . . . Sounds fake, but, okay."

"Goddess, what if it was a fake name?" Julian began to worry, biting at his nails. "Do you think it could have been some kind of prank? Who would even do that?" Burying his face in his hands, Julian groaned. "Oh, I bet he's laughing at me right now!"

"All right, all right!" Sami whined, putting up their hands. "Just take a breath or something!" They gave Julian a gentle shove before reaching into their bag to pull out a pack of smokes. Their thin, brown fingers placed a cigarette between their teeth, staining the edge of the filter with their lipstick. "You all right if I smoke?"

Before Julian could answer, a familiar voice called out from behind them. "Hey there, cuties!" The greeting was followed by the sound of heels clacking against pavement.

Sami turned and waved. "Hey, Paris!"

Julian clenched up and bit at the edge of his thumbnail. Paris gave Sami a hug hello before she turned to Julian, leaning down to kiss his cheek.

"Hi," Julian said meekly.

"What a party last night!" Paris gleefully exclaimed, winking at Julian. Sami shot a look back and forth between them while Julian shuffled his feet.

There was a pause before Paris shrugged and announced, "Well, I'm off! Meeting up with my mom for that big march thingie." She ran a hand over Julian's arm and gave a squeeze, adding, "I'm looking forward to Friday." With that, she was gone.

"Friday?" Sami asked with a grin.

"Yeah." Julian groaned. "Paris asked me out. I said yes."

Sami's jaw dropped, their cigarette dangling. "No! She went for it, eh? And you said yes?! Damn!" Sami's eyes glanced back toward the direction Paris had walked in. "She's so cool. . ." they murmured under their breath.

"I didn't know how to say no," Julian sighed. He bit down hard on his thumbnail, causing a crack to form along the edge. "Maybe I should just go back to bed, forever," he moaned.

Before Sami could try to talk Julian out of going home, another voice called out to them. "Heya, homos!" This time it was from the other side of the street.

Julian looked over to see a familiar face. "Looks like she's Guyna today," he remarked. Julian and Sami's friend wore a touch of red lipstick, had her hair pushed forward, and sported a low-cut shirt showing off her cleavage — all signs she usually used to indicate her gender-feels for the day. Sure enough, as she drew closer, Julian could see the nametag on his friend's work vest displaying the name 'Guyna' rather than 'Guy.'

Guyna greeted Sami with a playful punch and ruffled Julian's hair. Julian grumbled and leaned back, trying to fix his bangs. Sami, rubbing their arm, smirked up at Guyna and said, "Hey, you, did you know there's a little crepe hair on your chin?"

Guyna moved a hand to her face, feeling the prickly pasted-on hair. "Guess I had a bit left over from going Guy-mode to Lyla's party last night. Can't believe I just worked a whole shift and no one said a thing!" She let out a cackle before turning to Julian. "I heard you had a wild night!"

Julian glanced up, suddenly excited. Was it possible Guyna knew Romeo? Of all people, she was the one with the most connections to the hetero-flexible boys in the city. She practically made a sport of sleeping with them, especially when he was presenting as Guy!

"Rumour is you had a run-in with one of those haters who tried to crash," she said.

Julian sighed — that told him enough. She'd probably never even met the guy, let alone knew how to get a hold of him. He still had no leads on that mysterious midnight man.

Sami elbowed Julian. "Turns out that crasher's the man of Julian's wet dreams!"

"No shit!" Guyna exclaimed. Then she said, with more than a glint of pride, "I tangoed with one of 'em too. The awkward one, total brace-face, clearly a little closet case. Just my type!" She let out a snort.

"Started putting my moves on him. He didn't know what hit him! I swear, I thought he was gonna turn into a puddle at my feet!" She let out a roaring laugh, clearly pleased with herself.

Suddenly, a rumbling sound disrupted their conversation. A crowd was flowing toward them from the end of the street. They were chanting indistinct slogans and carrying picket signs. As they grew closer, Julian groaned. "Good Goddess, there's my mom!"

His friends started to laugh as they saw that, yes, there was Julian's mother, holding up a big banner at the front of a growing protest march. Julian couldn't believe he'd forgotten — his mom had been on about this for weeks. She was part of some new committee, and today she and her fellow activists were drumming up support for their cause.

"Hey, there's Paris!" Guyna exclaimed. Sure enough, there she was. When Paris spied the trio, she waved at them to come over and join the crowd.

"Is that her mom?" asked Sami. They motioned to another woman who looked almost like a twin to

Paris, just a few decades older.

Julian nodded. "My mom says she works at some school out in the 'burbs. She's the one who came up with this whole idea. She's trying to get some class on gender and sexuality or something into all the high schools."

"Wow," Sami whispered in awe.

"Can you imagine having a mom that cool?" Guyna added.

Julian just shrugged. He didn't have to imagine. In fact, he was trying not to think about it.

Sami got up and started making their way toward the crowd. Guyna quickly followed. Julian could think of few things more uncomfortable than putting himself in a big group of people drawing the attention of bigots, cops, politicians, and press. A pang of guilt hit him in the chest, but it wasn't strong enough to overpower the anxiety that buzzed through his body. Moving in the opposite direction, Julian yanked off his hangnail as he made his way to the bus stop.

05 Second Blush

JULIAN TAPPED HIS FEET AS HE LOOKED over the bus schedule. "Why are all the buses in Winnipeg always late?" he whined, peering down the street.

"You didn't seriously think you could get away that easy." Spinning around, Julian saw Sami, a smirk on their face. Guyna stood a half-step behind, with a hand on her hip.

Julian pouted. "I just don't like crowds." He crossed his arms. Lyla would have known that.

Sami shrugged. "Fair enough. Still, it was *you* that asked *me* to help get you out of the house. And since you pretty much only leave your bed, what . . ." Sami counted off a few fingers. "About once every four billion years?" They laughed. "I'm not letting you off that easy."

Julian sighed in defeat. He had thought that was what he wanted, a friend to get him out of his funk. But the outside world was too loud, too bright, and too dangerous.

"I think I know a good place for us to go," Guyna suggested. She scooped up Julian's arm and dragged him along. Julian looked back for just a moment and saw the bus approaching from the distance. He muttered a curse in its direction as he was pulled from the stop.

As they made their way to Guyna's mystery destination, Julian's stomach began to twist up with nerves. Sami and Guyna carried him along, keeping up their own conversation. Guyna was going on about her favourite subject — her recent sex-capades. Sami listened with excitement, asking questions, cracking sarcastic comments, and squealing with laughter, making Guyna's grin all the wider. Julian let himself slip from their grasp and follow a step behind the pair, thankful at least that his friends (or, at the moment, kidnappers) could keep each other occupied.

Julian started looking around. He caught one of the drivers on the street giving their trio a long look. A passing group of pedestrians let out a cruel-sounding giggle. Chewing the ends of his fingernails, Julian again found himself dreaming of the safety of his dark little bedroom. But it was too late to bail now. They had arrived — at The Orchard bookstore.

The Orchard was quiet and calm, just like Guyna had promised. With few other people in the store, Julian could wander among the dusty old paperbacks and look at their cover art. Guyna had barely taken two steps inside before she started putting the moves on the clerk behind the counter.

"Did you bring us here just to flirt?" Sami asked with a sideways smile. Guyna winked in response.

Julian's eyes fell on a book with a picture of a tall, handsome man, the romantic figure's dark hair swirling as he was silhouetted by a sunset. The character, to Julian, was the spitting image of Romeo. He picked it up and took in the details. He only glanced up when he realized Sami was standing next to him, giving a knowing look.

"I know, I know," Julian whined. He put the book back on the shelf in hurried embarrassment. "It's silly. But I just keep thinking about him!" He sighed. "Maybe I should just go home and do a painting. I need to get out this energy!"

"I can think of better ways to get out my energy!" Guyna responded loudly from the front of the store.

Sami shrugged and patted Julian on the shoulder. They left him to his fantasies, moving toward the back of the store to a section with books on body modification. Julian picked up the romance novel once more to look at the cover. He sighed, put it back down again, and moved deeper into the stacks.

Running his hand along the multi-coloured spines

of worn, second-hand books, Julian's mind returned to the night before. He relived the electricity of the kiss, the heartbreak of Romeo leaving without a goodbye. He was gripped with the fear that it had been, at best, a one-time chance encounter and, at worst, some kind of cruel joke.

"Romeo," Julian said the name quietly to himself. He liked the way it moved through his mouth, how it rolled off his tongue and fell through his lips. "Romeo," he said again. "Who is named Romeo these days, anyway? And what am I doing wanting a guy like that?" With a sigh, he said the name again. "Romeo . . . why did you run off like that? Was Ty right to chase you away? Were those guys really your friends? And what about me? Was I just a victim of a prank? Or a drunken experiment?" Julian leaned back onto a stack of books. "Romeo, who are you? Will I ever see you again?"

Out of the corner of his eye, Julian saw a row of books burst forward off the shelf. Several volumes fell to the floor. He approached with caution. Was there some kind of creeper in the stacks? Or maybe The Orchard had a ghost? Either way, his stomach clenched in embarrassment. What if someone had overheard him talking to himself? Just as suddenly as the books had fallen, a face appeared in the space. A face Julian recognized right away.

"You!" Julian and the face gasped in unison. Julian's jaw dropped. What were the chances? Romeo's face was framed by books, a deep red running up his cheeks. His wide eyes looked down, suddenly shy.

"Romeo, that's you, isn't it?" Julian asked, taking a step closer.

"I, um — it's, um —" Romeo stuttered a reply.

Julian smiled. He went to the edge of the small hole Romeo had made between the books. "I'm Julian," he offered. He put his hand on the edge of the opening, trying to lean in a little more. "Julian Capulet."

Romeo didn't meet Julian's eye. Instead, his gaze only got as far as Julian's fingertips. "What needed yellow?" Romeo asked.

"Hm?" Julian glanced down to where Romeo was looking. "Oh, that," Julian laughed. A splash of yellow was wrapped around the side of his pinky finger. "I was just doing a little painting. Guess I didn't wash it all off."

Romeo said something back, but Julian couldn't listen. He was too focused on Romeo's lips. He loved the way they looked as he spoke, moving back and forth like two dancers, coming together and apart again. They seemed warm and inviting. And they were getting closer . . . Julian leaned forward, close enough to feel Romeo's breath pushing up against his own, their faces hidden in a little cave made of books. It smelled like well-worn pages, old glue holding together spines of well-loved stories. There was just a touch of dust along the top of the larger novels. Julian took a deep breath. His fingertips gently reached out and touched Romeo's. Julian felt the same uncontrollable pull as the night before.

Romeo whispered, a nervous tremor in his voice, "Would you mind if I tested something?"

Julian nodded, absentmindedly. Now that their lips were so close, he was unable to think of anything else beyond the pounding of his heart as it filled up his head. Finally, Romeo leaned a centimetre closer, saying, "I sort of haven't really — I haven't felt the way I felt when we . . . I guess, I want to be sure." Then, at last, they connected in a kiss, and there was no need for words anymore.

A wave ran all the way through Julian's body. All he wanted was more. Nothing else mattered, nothing but this. He reached in to pull Romeo's face closer as their kiss became more passionate. They managed to knock over several more books in the process.

"Hey, you two!" the shopkeeper's voice rang out, interrupting their moment. "Not in the books, would ya?"

Julian's heart sank as Romeo pulled away and glanced toward the front of the store with a nervous look.

"Hey, is that you, Julian? Who you got there?" Guyna's voice came over in a shout from the direction

Romeo was looking. Julian whirled around and saw Sami approaching from the other side, looking curious, carrying an armful of books on DIY piercings and stick-n-poke tattoos.

Julian glanced back again at Romeo, who was breathing heavily. Not in the mood for his friends' probing questions and cutting remarks, Julian figured Romeo seemed just as anxious, maybe even more so. Without another thought, Julian ran to the end of the bookshelf. Grabbing Romeo's hand, he pulled him towards the door, heading out of The Orchard and into the street.

06 *I Like You*

JULIAN'S HIGH-TOPS HIT THE PAVEMENT, followed by the clap of Romeo's skate shoes. Julian glanced back at him, flashing a smile. "Come on," he said, squeezing Romeo's hand. "I know a place."

They ran past bars, restaurants, cafés, and corner stores. Neon lights and streetlamps buzzed awake. Normally, Julian would be anxious to get home by now. But with Romeo at his side, he almost felt safe. They passed out of Osborne Village, cut through the park outside the city legislature, and entered the heart of downtown. Barely a word passed between the two as Julian weaved them through the streets, clutching Romeo's hand tightly, only glancing back once in a while to make sure this was really happening. He was really there. Soon enough, they reached the Exchange District. Julian led Romeo to a place he'd loved to visit, back in the days before he pulled away from the outside world — The Hungry Rhino.

Inside, things were fairly quiet. Julian's old favourite table was open, the one near the back with a chessboard print painted on it. The pair set themselves down into the well-worn wooden chairs and, after a few minutes of avoiding eye contact, Julian began to nervously bite his fingernails. While they were walking, the quiet had been comfortable. But now the lack of conversation was awkward. What if they had nothing in common? What if Julian had just ditched his friends, without even telling them where he was going, to sit down face-to-face with a stranger and potential homophobe?

Impulsively, Julian blurted out, "This is one of my favourite restaurants!" Letting out a laugh, he added, "Goddess, that makes me sound like such a dork, right? But it's really cool — I promise. They have all this organic, local, vegetarian stuff. Did I mention my mom is vegetarian? And, so, I am too, pretty much, I guess. Oh, and they share all the work in this place in a really cool way — like nobody's the owner. Like kind of a commune? They switch jobs every few weeks so everyone has to wash the dishes at least sometimes!" Julian found he was going on and on, unable to stop, only pausing to nervously giggle. He was totally losing his cool. Finally, he looked up to find that Romeo wasn't even looking at him.

Romeo's eyes were glancing all around the restaurant, taking in the other tables and reading the menu scrawled on the wall in chalk. Julian coughed, cutting himself short. He took a moment to glance at the food options too, even though he knew them well.

Silence sat between them, again, broken only by brief talk about what they might like to eat. Julian hopped up to place their order at the counter. When he sat back down, Romeo had a confession.

"I'm not exactly . . . *out*," Romeo admitted, in nearly a whisper.

Julian raised an eyebrow. It was an odd place to start a conversation, but there they were.

"So, when did you, uh . . ." Romeo went on, "decide? Or, like, know . . . you know?" He stumbled over his words.

Julian shrugged. "Well, it's easier when your mom's out before you are."

"What?" Romeo asked.

"My mom's been doing activist stuff my whole life. She was out as bi before I was even born! My cousin too, he's had a couple boyfriends . . ." Julian trailed off as his thoughts turned to Ty. What would Ty think if he saw Julian on a date with one of the guys he'd kicked out of Lyla's party not even twenty-four hours earlier?

"So, were you raised to be gay?"

"I don't really like labels," Julian replied.

"But you like guys, right?" Romeo asked, a little hesitant.

"I like people," Julian replied. "I like you." Taking a deep breath, he fought against his nerves and asked, "What about you?"

"What about me?" Romeo asked back. Julian raised an eyebrow and Romeo smirked, blushing a little. "I guess . . . I like you?"

Just then, their order number was called, and Julian jumped to the counter, bringing back plates of hot, delicious-looking food to the table — one order of deep fried tofu, and one "B"LT.

"So what's your dad like?" Romeo asked, poking at his meal. "Is he, uh, like your mom?"

Julian winced. "I don't really know," he answered, pushing his food around. "My mom doesn't like to talk about him. My cousin used to, sometimes, but we haven't really talked in a while . . ." Julian looked down as a wave of anxiety squeezed his gut. Just who was this boy anyway? Who did he think he was, asking all these questions — they barely knew each other!

Did he really expect Julian just to open up and lay it all out there? A pang of guilt hit his chest. His thoughts racing, Julian mumbled, "I just miss him."

"Who, your dad?" Romeo asked.

Julian shook his head. "No. I mean, yes. But no, I mean my cousin." With a sigh, he figured there was no point in holding back. Maybe it would be nice to talk to someone who didn't know the rest of his friends and family. "He's from my dad's side, but I don't really know his parents either. I think his mom was my dad's sister? Anyway, we used to be really close. He'd come over, make up games, tell me stories, that sort of thing." With a laugh, he added, "And he'd always stay for dinner! I don't think my mom liked that too much. But she wasn't about to turn down a free babysitter! She was still in school to be a nurse back then."

Romeo nodded with understanding. After a moment, he cautiously asked, "So what happened to him?"

Julian bit his lip, picking apart pieces of his food without thinking. "He got locked up," Julian admitted. Romeo didn't look like he understood, so Julian explained, "Corrections."

Romeo was silent.

Julian looked up, studying the ceiling. "I used to write him letters. I kept saying I'd come visit. But I never did get down there in person."

"I'm sure he understands," Romeo offered in a gentle voice.

"He's out now," Julian explained. "But we haven't really had a chance to talk." He looked down at the table, studying the scratches that stood out against the checkerboard design. "I just . . . I don't know."

Wordlessly, Romeo leaned forward and offered his hand. Julian looked up and accepted it, the warmth of Romeo's touch bringing him back to the moment. They sat in comfortable silence for a while.

Julian ran his thumb along the edge of Romeo's hand. "It's nice to talk about this stuff." He smiled softly and added, "It's nice to be with you."

Romeo began to blush again.

07 Raised Eyebrows

THE EVENING RAN ON. Not wanting their time together to end, Julian impulsively invited Romeo to go home with him. On their way, they dared to share a quick kiss in public. The act sent shivers of both fear and excitement through Julian's body. When they arrived at his house, those feelings began to flutter in his stomach once again.

They went through the old wooden gate which, as usual, hung open — the lock had broken long ago.

They made their way along the cracked sidewalk, up the creaking porch stairs, and arrived at the chipped paint on the front door.

"It's . . ." Julian bit at his bottom lip. "Probably not like the kind of homes you're used to in the suburbs." He watched Romeo out of the corner of his eye, waiting for some snide remark. Things were going too well. There had to be some nasty side to this guy that Julian just hadn't seen yet. Maybe now Romeo would reveal his true snobby self.

Romeo paused. Julian fiddled with his keys, bracing for the worst. Finally, Romeo asked, "Did you make that?"

Julian followed Romeo's gaze to the mural on the front of the house. It was so old and familiar Julian often forgot it was even there. "Mostly it was my mom," he answered. His mind went back to the days he'd spent outside with her. Back when things seemed just a little warmer, when summer lasted just a little longer. His mom laughed more then, teasing Ty when he'd come around. Looking over at the mural, lit up only by the lights from the street, Julian remembered the way his mother had made the swirling stars, teaching him how to pull the brush without dripping the paint. And there were Julian's doodles along the edges, with his name signed next to his mom's, at the bottom. Looking up at Romeo, Julian saw him taking in the piece with awe. Watching him see the mural for the first time, felt kind of like Julian was seeing it for the first time, too. "It's pretty cool, I guess," Julian admitted. He turned the key in the door and motioned for Romeo to follow him inside.

Julian had barely taken a step in when a voice called out from the kitchen. "Is that my boy?!"

"Mom!" Julian answered. "You're home!"

Julian's mother burst into the hall, stretching her arms out toward her son and wrapping him in a big hug. "Oh, my darling jewel," she said, squeezing him tightly.

Once his mom finally let him free, Julian motioned to Romeo standing awkwardly in the doorway. He offered a quick introduction. "Mom, this is Romeo. I'm having him over tonight."

Romeo gave a timid wave and Julian's mother responded with a nod.

"What kind of a name is Romeo?" she asked in a loud, comedic whisper. Julian smirked and followed her back toward the kitchen. Romeo was just a step behind.

"Oh, Jules, today was fantastic!" she crowed. "We made such a stink, I bet you anything we made it onto national news!"

"Right, the demonstration . . ." Julian replied. He was taking in the warmth of the kitchen — a wonderful smell was in the air.

"Joanna was there, of course, with her girl Paris. They are such an adorable pair!" She leaned over and gave Julian a teasing pinch before pulling on her oven mitts. "Now, if only my little darling had been there too!" She turned away, pulling a tray of fresh brownies out of the oven. The sweet smell of chocolate filled up the whole room. Julian leaned in to try and grab a bite but his hands were shooed away.

"These are hot!" his mother scolded. Setting the

brownies on the stove, she added, "Besides, they're not for you. Not unless you plan on showing up tomorrow night. We've got a lot to do before Saturday's demo, this time we're going even bigger!" She nudged him. "We could really use you at the planning meeting."

Julian just shrugged. His mom knew he'd rather avoid all that political stuff. "We'll see," he replied.

"I'll get you one of these days — you'll see. By the time you're my age, you'll be the one planning the revolution, while I put my feet up at home!" Julian shrugged again. "Fine, fine," his mother relented. She motioned to the dishes in the sink. "Now, Jules, would you and your friend be dears and wash these for me?"

Julian plucked a large, wooden spoon covered in brownie mix from the sink. He took a lick before offering some to Romeo, who chose to pass. Julian started to fill the sink with hot, soapy water. "Got much experience washing dishes?" he asked. Romeo just blushed in response. Julian passed him a drying cloth and the two got to work.

After a while, Romeo spoke up. "It's, uh, nice to meet you, Mrs. Capulet."

Julian winced. He could feel his mother prickle at the sound of his father's name. Back when he was in public school, teachers had often made that same mistaken assumption. His mother had quickly corrected them each time. Thankfully, she'd never pressured Julian to change his name, though he was sure she wouldn't mind if he took her last name instead. But the name was one of the few things his father had left behind. Julian wasn't about to let it go, even if it made things awkward sometimes.

"You can call me Angie, Angie Liang," his mother replied to Romeo.

Julian looked from Romeo to his mother, wondering how this all must look in Romeo's eyes. Back when Julian was at school, lots of kids and even teachers had made snide remarks about his mother. Somebody had even started a rumour that Julian was adopted, or even stolen, being raised by a dangerous "bull-dyke."

His mother was fabulously fat, broad shouldered, and tall. With beautiful, bronze skin, her wide face was framed by a crew-cut that she bleached and dyed bright violet. On her days off from the hospital, she wrapped herself in bright shirts with radical slogans, or sported her pin-covered denim vest, using every bit of her body to make a statement. She was easily in command of any room, unafraid to speak her mind or step out to the front of a picket line.

Julian let a lock of his straight, dark hair fall in front of his face. He scrubbed the large pot in the sink, his hands pruning in the hot water. Compared to his mother, he felt small, and unsure of himself. His shorter stature and anxious disposition marked him as his father's child. At least that's what Ty had told him, back in the day.

After a while, Angie seemed to warm up a little to Romeo — at least enough to leave him be. But that meant she turned her attention back to Julian, asking, "So, get your grades yet?"

"Incomplete," Julian admitted, pretending to focus on the dishes.

Angie pursed her lips and raised her eyebrows at him, waiting for more.

Julian sighed. He hadn't wanted to get into this in front of Romeo. "Pretty much, I failed. They said I 'deviated from the assignments.'"

His mother frowned, and looked like she was about to plan her next protest. Julian just looked down at the soapy water again.

Angie put a hand on her hip with a snort, declaring, "Well, what do they know anyway!" She leaned over and gave Julian a quick kiss on his forehead.

"Yeah." He shrugged. "They did say I could try a make-up, redo the final essay. So long as I don't deviate too much . . ." He looked to his mother, hoping she might know what to do. Was it really worth it to risk failing again?

As if reading his mind, she answered, "It's up to you then, jewel." Nudging her hip into him, she added, "Sounds like you're just too smart for that system."

Julian looked up and let out a little laugh. At least she was supportive.

After dishes were done, Julian pulled Romeo out of the kitchen and upstairs. On his way out, he reached over and nabbed a handful of brownies. Within a moment, Angie called after him, "Oh, Goddess — Julian!" She laughed, "Well, you are my son after all."

Julian grinned and continued upstairs. As they reached the top, his mother called out once more. "You know where the condom jar is!"

"The condom jar?" Romeo asked.

"Mom's a very sex-positive feminist," Julian replied, pulling Romeo into his attic bedroom.

08 Bottle Up this Moment

AS USUAL, JULIAN'S ROOM WAS CHAOS. He hadn't
found the energy to tidy up, and it had been like this
for so long now he didn't care much anymore. He
just let things drop where they may and searched for
whatever he needed among the varying piles. There
was art stuff in one part of the room, clothing shoved
near the closet, shoes in a jumble by the door. Julian
braced himself for embarrassment. He tried to subtly
move some things on the floor around with his feet,

clearing a path so they could at least sit on the bed. Romeo barely seemed to notice, too taken with the posters on Julian's walls and the canvases set up on the far side of the room. After a while, Romeo declared, "This is wonderful." Julian somehow felt even more embarrassed than if Romeo had made a comment about the mess.

As they sat on the bed, Julian became intimately aware of how close Romeo's body was to his own. How nice it might be just to cuddle with someone again. It had been a long time since he'd trusted anyone enough to get this close. There was a faint buzzing in his belly, but it was almost nice, like the feeling he got when he painted.

Julian was studying Romeo's face when he spoke up. "Your mom seems cool."

Julian looked up at the ceiling. "Yeah, she's cool, that's for sure." Romeo gave him an odd look, so Julian went on. "It's just . . . sometimes it's like she's too cool." Julian felt tired just thinking about everything she did. "Like, she's got all these stories to tell, and projects on the go. And somehow finds the energy to work all those long shifts at the hospital."

"It's just the two of you, right?" Romeo said his question like a statement.

Julian nodded. "It can be lonely sometimes, when she's not around." A soft, sad kind of smile crossed his face. "But then, when she's around all the time, it can get to be too much! Funny how that is . . ."

Romeo let his hand brush up against Julian's, sending a shiver between the two of them. He broached another question. "Did you ever know your dad?"

Julian shrugged, looking down to study the paint speckled on the floor of his room. "Mom doesn't talk about him too much. I never really got to know him. I don't even really know what he looks like."

"I'm sorry," Romeo said. "You don't even have a picture or anything? That . . . sucks."

Julian sighed. "My cousin Ty used to tell me about him, sometimes. Apparently they kinda look alike, Ty and my dad — both redheads, though you wouldn't know it since Ty never lets his hair grow in. Plus, Ty says he's like, five times bigger than my dad ever was!" Julian let out a little laugh.

"That's pretty rough," Romeo said. He gently ran his hand over Julian's arm, making the hair stand on end. "No memories of your own . . . Always getting the stories about him second-hand."

"But I do remember him!" Julian exclaimed, looking up to Romeo. "Like from when I was really little." Julian pulled on those distant memories, foggy as they were. "I remember him singing to me." He smiled. "I even remember, he had a nickname for me — his little fawn, I think." Romeo smiled and gave a small nod, lightly squeezing Julian's arm.

Conversation fell away and the couple leaned back onto the bed, basking in their closeness. Julian loved the smell of Romeo, the taste of him — everything about him was so exciting. He drank Romeo in, every single part of him. His mop of thick, dark hair that twisted between Julian's fingers. The touch of his fingertips lightly brushing against

Julian's skin. The salty-sweetness of his neck as Julian ran his lips up that strong jawline.

Julian was amazed at how Romeo could hold his attention, and it wasn't just his body. As much as it was tempting to just get lost staring at that cute face, Julian found himself entranced as Romeo began to open up about his own family, and his own scars. Julian listened intently as he traced a harsh scar that ran from the base of Romeo's palm up to the finger where Romeo sported his class ring.

At last, standing to turn off the lights, Julian took a deep breath and decided it was time — he was ready. "You shared your scars with me," he began, undoing the top of his jeans.

"I've never . . ." Romeo whispered.

Julian nodded. Kneeling alongside Romeo, he took the young man's hand and put it just below his boxer-briefs. Romeo ran his fingers against the thin scars along Julian's thighs, tracing the cuts Julian had made on the nights when it had been too hard to carry on.

Finally, Julian let go, falling back into Romeo's arms. Tears began to push up and out of him. He was no longer able to hold anything back. With Romeo holding him tightly, he found the memories and nightmares again. But this time he could say them out loud.

"I-I just —" Julian struggled to put all his feelings into words. "When I tried to go to school . . . things just . . . they were hard. Every — everybody said my mom was a dyke. That she stole me. Or that she drove my dad away, or made him kill himself . . ." Julian choked on his words. "They told me to kill myself," he said at last.

Romeo said nothing. After a moment, as Julian took a few deep breaths, he found his words again. "Then . . . some of them started to follow me home. They'd call me names, throw stuff at me. Somebody even tried to run me down in the school parking lot!" Julian squeezed Romeo. If he held on, he wouldn't get sucked back into those memories and the blank, empty pit that hung below them. "It was just brutal," he managed, burying his head in Romeo's chest.

Julian felt dry, empty, and tired. "After all that," he said with a sniffle, "I just didn't want to go out anymore. I dropped out of school — out of life. I couldn't even get out of bed." Julian couldn't look at Romeo as he told this part. But he couldn't hold it back either. "Mom had to take time off work and take care of me. I was just this . . . broken thing. A burden. And when she wasn't around, I was just alone." Julian sighed, too tired to care about the anxiety or guilt anymore. "I couldn't bring myself to talk to my friends. It just felt . . . impossible. Even just to answer the phone. And my cousin, he was locked up. I couldn't even bring myself to leave the house and go see him. All I could do was write him letters sometimes. And even then, all I did was complain about my own life." Julian clung to Romeo like a life-preserver in a stormy sea. "I felt like such a failure. And so selfish for pitying myself." Finally, out of breath, he whispered, "I just wanted to die."

Romeo held Julian closely. He breathed into his hair and whispered back, "I'm glad you kept going. I'm glad you're here now."

They began to kiss again. Julian felt raw, more exposed than he'd been in years — maybe more than he'd ever been. And Romeo was clearly nervous, unused to all this, but open, and wanting to be there. His kisses were messy, sometimes awkward, but he made up for it in passion, gripping at Julian's hips and pulling him closer. Skin against skin, breath into breath, Julian fell into Romeo's embrace and let the rest of the world fade away.

Hands explored shoulders, backs arched and fell, their bodies pushed against each other. There was even some hair pulling. Julian wondered if he should stop what was happening before they went any further. Or maybe they should make a run to the condom jar?

Finally, they pulled apart, breathing heavily. They paused to just look at each other. In the darkness, Julian found he could be seen, heard, held — all without judgement. Maybe this could work after all. Maybe he could finally let someone in.

Exhausted, the pair curled up together. They held on to each other as if the world could slip away at any second. Julian wished he could just bottle up that moment and live in it forever.

09 What Is Love?

"I'M FINE, MOM, I'M FINE!" Romeo protested. Julian groggily woke. He rolled over to see Romeo, still topless and half under the covers, speaking into his phone. "I know. I'm sorry . . ."

Julian grinned and pushed himself up. He ran his fingers along Romeo's exposed skin, making the hairs on Romeo's neck stand up.

Romeo started to blush and his voice wavered. "I-I-I have some errands to run."

Julian's hands went exploring further. He began to kiss along Romeo's neck, making him squirm.

"I don't know when I'll be back. Maybe ten tonight?"

Julian could hear the voice of a woman on the other end of the phone. She did not sound pleased.

"Okay! Okay! I'll be home for dinner! God!" Romeo managed, trying to wrap up the call. "I'll talk to you later. Mom . . . Yeah of course. You too." Romeo groaned. "I don't want to say it. I'm in front of the guys!"

Julian started to giggle.

"Okay, okay! I love you too! Goodbye!" Romeo nearly shouted. He ended the call just in time, before Julian broke into a laughing fit. "Oh my God!" Romeo shouted, playfully pushing Julian off of him and back onto the bed.

They skipped down the stairs for breakfast. Julian smiled with every step. "You know," he mused, whipping up banana pancakes for their breakfast, "A part of me was worried you were just a good dream —

that I'd wake up, and you'd be gone again."

Romeo grinned, plates and cutlery in his hands. "Well, here I am!"

Julian snuck a quick kiss on Romeo's cheek. "Yeah, here you are."

Chatting away, they spread peanut butter and jam on their pancakes, since there was no maple syrup in the house. Angie was nowhere in sight. Julian assumed she was back at work already, or maybe a planning meeting for whatever big political thing she was working on this week.

"What should we do today?" Romeo asked. With sun pouring through the windows, Julian could tell it was going to be a beautiful day. Normally, no matter the weather, he would have found an excuse to stay inside. But with Romeo here, the outside world seemed more appealing.

"How about we start with a walk?" Julian offered, as he cleared the dishes from the table. "My mom started this community garden in an old lot a couple streets over. We could go check it out."

Romeo grinned widely and nodded.

As they stepped outside, Romeo looked around. Julian waited for him to say something about the boarded up house across the street, or the potholes along the road. Romeo was nice, but he'd probably never even been this far from his sheltered little cul-de-sac. "I think it's beautiful here." Romeo beamed at Julian, speaking with such sincerity that Julian started to feel his face grow hot in embarrassment.

The community garden was starting to bloom. A few buds poked their way up through the wet soil. Romeo looked over the small lot with amazement. "You did this?" he asked.

"Well, mostly my mom," Julian assured him. "I helped a little . . . I guess."

An older woman was weeding. She raised her head to give a wary look at the two teenagers — and then she realized who it was.

"Oh, Julian!" she called out. She gave him a big wave and a wide, toothy smile.

Julian gave a shy wave back. "Hi, Summer!"

"How's your mother?!" The woman shouted her question, not pausing in her uprooting of unwanted bits of green and yellow.

"Working hard, as always!" Julian answered.

Summer gave a nod back, a tuft of grey hair falling from underneath her wide sunhat. "And who's that with you?"

"This is Romeo!" Julian sang out.

At the same time, Romeo replied, "I'm Rome!"

Summer scrunched up her nose and turned her head. "Well, which is it?"

Romeo and Julian looked at one another and just shrugged.

"All right . . ." she said, turning her sunhat down. "Well, you have a nice day now!"

As they walked away, Romeo asked, "How old were you when your mom made the garden?"

"I don't know," Julian shrugged. "Maybe eight or nine."

Romeo blushed and quickly kissed Julian's cheek. "I'm just picturing you, playing in the dirt, helping plant those seeds. I bet you've always been cute."

They made their way around through alleys, admiring the clovers growing up between the cracks in the sidewalk, pausing to appreciate the graffiti on the backs of buildings. As they passed by the old cemetery, Romeo tripped, catching his foot on a hole in the sidewalk and falling face-first. Blushing wildly, he rushed to get up, while Julian reached down and offered a hand. Romeo turned an even deeper shade of red as he accepted the offer. Even after Julian pulled him up, they didn't let go.

The backstreets eventually took them toward the nearest main road. They stopped for lunch at a diner, holding hands over the table as they sipped afternoon coffee. It was scary to be so public with their affection. But Julian found he was glancing over his shoulder less and less. His heart was beating a little more steadily too. Taking a deep breath, he studied Romeo's face and marvelled at just how comfortable it felt to be so close to someone.

"What're you thinking right now?" Julian asked, sipping his tea.

Romeo shrugged. Julian gave him a minute, and he admitted, "Well, it's just . . . you know that feeling we have right now?" He looked down. "That feeling of, uh, falling for someone?"

Julian gave a little smile. "Yeah?"

"I mean, it's just chemicals in our brain, right?" Romeo looked out the window, not seeming to focus on anything. "That's what they said in school. Dopamine, and probably serotonin, making us think we're in love." He blushed at the word, adding, "Or whatever."

"So?" Julian ran a finger along Romeo's palm.

"So, I mean, if you think about it, love doesn't really exist," Romeo said. He looked serious, puzzled. "We just trick ourselves into thinking it does."

"I think people think too little of chemicals," Julian replied. Romeo gave him a curious look. "I mean, if you think about it that way, every thought and emotion and idea anyone has ever had is just chemicals sloshing around in their brain. But even if that was true, why does that make it any less real?"

Romeo shrugged, and Julian went on. "Personally, I think there's more, too. Like, our brain is just a little part of it. We've got a heart, hands, a whole body. And other people's bodies!" Julian raised an eyebrow, making Romeo blush. "And all kinds of stuff that science can't explain. Like, my mom's a witch, right? So she's taught me about magic, souls, spirits, all kinds of different rituals, spells, meditations, and medicines. But even if you want to say all that stuff is chemicals too, so what? The whole universe is made up of tiny little atoms and electrons and who-knows-what!" Julian grinned. "Isn't that what makes it amazing?"

"You're brilliant, you know that?" Romeo asked with a smile.

Tracing his fingers up Romeo's arm, Julian replied with a wink. "Probably just my brain chemicals."

They spent their afternoon at the diner, slowly sipping their hot drinks. Eventually, the pair made their way home, walking along the busy street and peering into the shops. Julian was just pointing the way back to his house when there was the sharp sound of car tires and a loud voice calling out to them. The words were gone too fast for Julian to hear. But the anger, disgust, and threat in the voice were clear enough.

Romeo jumped and took off running. He yanked Julian down the street at a shocking speed, heading away from the car and toward Julian's street. Within a minute or so, they were heading up Julian's steps. But even after the door was firmly locked behind them, Romeo was bent double, breathing heavily, and his hands were shaking. "Hey, hey," Julian said, his own voice trembling. His heart pounded in his head, but he took a deep breath. "We're safe now."

Romeo hit himself in the head and shouted, "I'm so stupid!"

"What?" Julian asked. "Why?"

Romeo didn't say anything. His silence was its own answer. This was it, Julian was sure of it. This had all been too good to be true. Now Romeo would leave, and Julian would be all alone, again.

Julian looked down, dejected. "I'm sorry," he mumbled, unsure what else to say.

Romeo finally looked up. "No. It's my fault. It's just that . . . that used to be me. Pretty recently."

This time, it was Julian who pulled away. Every mean-spirited remark, every cruel whisper ever thrown in his direction, raced through his mind. Julian was struck with a frightening realization. Romeo had admitted to hanging out with homophobes. But it was more than that, wasn't it? He was one of them. "Goddess," Julian whispered. Was Romeo just another bigoted bully? Was he just working out his homophobia, using Julian as his test subject?

Eventually, Romeo stood. "I should go."

Julian asked, on the edge of crying. "So that's it?"

Romeo looked back at Julian, tears in his eyes. "I'll be back. I promise."

10 *Backstab*

"IT'LL JUST BE A COUPLE OF HOURS," said Lyla. "You can come, right?"

Julian held the phone in one hand while he chewed on the thumbnail of the other. Holed up in his room, he stared at a blank document sitting open on his computer. He was trying to force himself to start the make-up assignment for his online class.

"Please," Lyla begged. "I miss you, Julian."

He sighed. How could he say no to that? "Fine. Sure. Yes," Julian replied, closing the laptop. "When should I be there?"

"Well, Ty's going to get the stuff with Harvey around three . . ." Lyla began.

Julian's stomach tightened. "Ty's gonna be there?"

"Yeah!" Lyla replied. "Harvey too. You've met him, right?"

Julian hadn't had a chance to get to know Ty's partner yet. "Mhm," was all Julian could think to say.

"Fabulous," said Lyla. "Ty and Harvey are picking up Rose and her stuff, around three. So if you want you could come by around four. Maybe four-thirty?"

Julian was only half listening. The sound of his pounding heart filled his head. Before he could say anything more, there was a sound on the other side of the line.

"Oh! Come on in!" Lyla called out. "Guy's here," she explained to Julian. "And he's early! And he's got food!" Julian could hear the faint voice of Guy saying something about leftovers from the diner. "I'll see you later!" Lyla chirped. And then she was gone.

Julian sat in his room, sulking. Ty and Lyla, at once? They were the two people who used to be his closest confidants. Now both felt like people he barely knew. "Great," he mumbled to himself. "Maybe I can disappoint them both at once."

♥ ♥ ♥

Julian stood at the door to Lyla's apartment, staring down the rainbow sticker below the peephole. "This'll be over soon enough," he said to himself. "How long can it really take to move a few boxes?"

He checked his phone. It had been a little less than a day since he'd seen Romeo. But all he could think of was how much he wanted them to be back in bed together, curled up, safe and sound. The thought calmed his heart a little, long enough for him to take a deep breath and knock.

It was Guy who opened the door, but he wasn't

wearing his usual wry grin. He ushered Julian inside. His brows were tight and he said little as he led Julian into the living room before heading to the kitchenette.

"And that's when he tackled me," Ty said to Lyla. Ty's partner Harvey was at his side, pressing an ice pack to the back of Ty's head, resting his spare hand on Ty's shoulder.

Lyla barely glanced at Julian. She motioned for him to sit down.

"Hey, Jules," Ty said. He managed a small smile in Julian's direction. Harvey gave Julian a little wave.

Julian looked around the room and then back at Ty. "What happened?"

"They got jumped!" Guy called out from the kitchen.

"What?!"

"We didn't get *jumped*," Ty corrected. "There was . . . an altercation." He was clearly choosing his words carefully.

Julian raised a brow and waited, hoping for a more detailed explanation.

With a sigh, Ty recounted his story. "Harvey and I were driving over to Rose's old place — over near Southdale? And I was going by the high school out there."

Julian nodded, following so far.

"So I saw a couple guys," Ty continued. "Guys I recognized. They had on those jackets — same ones those 'phobes wore to Lyla's thing on Friday."

Julian's stomach tightened.

"I knew it was them." Ty scowled. "I'd seen those guys before that, too, when they threw shit at me and Harvey from a car a week or so back. So, I guess, I was pretty pissed off. And I pulled over. I don't know what I thought I was gonna do. Talk to them, I guess." He shrugged. "But before I could say anything, they must have recognized me, too. They started shouting shit at me, trying to start a fight."

Ty looked up at Harvey. "It was just a waste of time, and we knew it. They just wanted to rile us up. We were just about to leave when one of them called us . . ." Ty sighed. "Fags." He spoke the word in a quiet, harsh tone.

"And then what?" Julian asked. "Did you hit him?"

Ty gave him a sad look. "Julian . . ." he said.

Julian's heart sank. He looked down, embarrassed he'd even asked. This was Ty! Sweet and good-natured, his sometimes babysitter, his storyteller, the link to Julian's father — he was family! But at the same time, looking at him now, Julian couldn't help but notice that Ty had changed. He was older than the version Julian held in his memories, and more serious. There was even a scar down the side of one cheek that Julian swore he hadn't had before. He wasn't so sure he knew this version of his cousin.

"They hit first," Ty sighed. "We had to defend ourselves."

Guy called out again. "It was three on one!" He spoke like a sports announcer. But Julian couldn't find it funny.

"You said it was just a couple?" Julian asked.

"Another guy came out of nowhere!" Ty replied.

"Harvey was keeping one off my back, while I got a swing in on the other." Ty held up his hand, showing a gash on his knuckles. "But then the third one just tackled me!" He motioned to the icepack still on the back of his head. "He knocked me down — hard, too. After that, Harvey got me up and out of there. And we came right back here."

"Do you think you should see a doctor?" offered Lyla.

"I've had worse." Ty shrugged.

"I just . . . I can't believe it . . ." Julian breathed, still shocked. "You're sure it was the same guys as the ones at Lyla's party?"

Ty nodded at Julian. "Definitely," he replied.

Julian's stomach did an uneasy flip.

"There was the mouthy one, the little one with braces, and that big guy with the bad hair. That was the one who did this to the back of my head!"

"Your sweet Romeo, Julian?" Guy asked, with more than a little snark, as he came into the room with a bowl of chopped fruit. "It's such a small queer world," he mused. He shoved a few strawberries into his mouth before setting the dish on the table.

"You know that guy?" Ty asked Julian.

Not waiting for Julian to reply, Guy burst in, "Yeah, Julian knows he's a closet-case, gay-bashing asslick! And not the good kind of asslick."

"You guys don't know him like I do," Julian said quietly.

"Didn't you say they were gonna call the cops on you?" asked Lyla. Ty nodded. The whole room hushed.

Julian looked back down at the ground, studying the carpet, tense with worry.

"Julian, get real. Aren't you supposed to go out with Paris, anyway?" Guy asked. "Why are you hanging out with that creep?"

Julian shook his head. His thoughts were too loud. This was too much. He stood and made his way to the door, saying simply, "I have to go."

11 Honesty

ANGIE WAS OUT. Maybe she was at work or maybe at one of her political meetings. At that moment, it didn't really matter to Julian.

"Thank the Goddess," he said to the empty house. He went upstairs to his paints.

The canvas stayed blank. Julian came at it from different angles. He tried every colour in his collection. He even put on some music for inspiration. But all of it did nothing but make him more anxious. Falling on his bed in frustration, Julian stared up at the ceiling.

He felt like he'd been the one punched in the face — or stabbed in the back. Nothing was ever going to get better, not after this.

"Maybe I should just give up on Romeo," he said. At this point, why not? He was probably never going to see Romeo again anyway. Julian pulled out his cell phone and saw he'd missed a few texts.

The first was from Paris, confirming their Friday plans. He shrugged. *Might as well go out with her*, he figured. *It must just be fate.*

The next was from Lyla, asking if he was all right. Julian hesitated, not sure what to say. She was probably still with Ty, Harvey, and Guy. They were probably all talking about him. How he was such an awful human being. How foolish he was for thinking he could ever trust a guy like Romeo.

No, he couldn't talk to Lyla about this. But he had to talk to someone. Julian moved to the second best option. He fired off a text to Sami — who called right away rather than texting back.

"Well?" Sami began.

Julian didn't respond.

"Have you talked to him yet?" asked Sami.

"Who?" Julian asked in return.

"Romeo, of course!"

Julian was silent again.

"I'm coming over," Sami announced, ending the call abruptly.

Julian barely had a moment to think before the doorbell rang. "How did they get here so soon?" Julian wondered aloud.

Getting up from his bed, Julian made his way to the window. He saw a car parked outside. His instincts told him it was Romeo's.

"Well I'm not gonna let him in," Julian said to himself, crossing his arms. "He can sit out there all night for all I care."

After a minute or two, Julian was biting his nails furiously. He glimpsed Romeo heading back to his car. Romeo rooted around for a while before coming back to the house and knocking even louder. Julian let out a sigh. Unable to help himself, he cautiously made his way downstairs.

Romeo didn't look good. He was shaking and sweating. He was running his hands through his hair and making it stick up at odd angles.

"I heard what happened," Julian said, his voice flat. He was shocked at his own tone. It was steady and direct, serious. Soon Romeo was little more than a puddle. Tears rolled down his cheeks and a dribble of snot peeked out of his nose.

Romeo mumbled an apology, looking positively pitiful. Julian resisted the urge to wrap him into a hug. Guilty tears were not going to fix anything. Still, not willing to let him just blubber on the front step, Julian pulled him inside.

Julian took a paint-stained cloth from his back pocket and offered it so Romeo could dry his tears. The colours on the rag transferred to Romeo's face, leaving little rainbow flecks on his flushed cheeks.

Julian couldn't stop thinking of Ty. How scary it had been to see him hurt. How frightening it was that

Romeo could do such a thing.

"How could you hurt someone like that?" Julian asked. "Did you really threaten to call the police?" His insides felt like a storm, but Julian found he remained strong and clear, at least on the outside.

Romeo winced. "I didn't know what to do."

Julian raised an eyebrow, sceptical.

"Honestly, I didn't even want to fight. When I got there, I was too late to stop it. And when I saw him hit Marty I just lost it. I think it was the blood — Marty's blood. It brought something out in me. I just . . . God, I wasn't thinking." Romeo sighed. "I'm so sorry . . ." he trailed off, putting his head in his hands.

"Romeo," Julian began, "that man you hurt, you'd seen him before, right? At the party?"

Romeo looked up and nodded a little.

"The thing is, that's Ty. My cousin." Julian went on as Romeo's eyes grew wide. "The other guy is his partner, Harvey."

Romeo looked down at his hands.

"It's bad enough you — or, at least, your friends — started a fight with him," Julian went on. He felt heat rising in his cheeks. "But threatening to call the police?" He shuddered, his voice faltering for the first time. "Romeo, he could be sent back to prison. Or worse . . ."

The two sat in silence. When, before, quiet moments together felt close, intimate, and comfortable, this time it was anything but. It was a long, tense silence. It clouded over all the other noises of the house and the street outside. Eventually, Romeo admitted, "I didn't know . . ."

"Clearly," Julian replied.

"I'm sorry," Romeo said desperately. He was still sweating and shaking a bit. *Maybe he's still in shock*, thought Julian.

"I don't need your apology."

Romeo tried to explain to Julian that it wasn't his idea. That he didn't even want to talk to the police. But Julian made it clear and simple. "If it was your friends, then talk your friends out of it," he said. "You could literally destroy Ty's life."

Romeo nodded. "Ben was the one who started everything. He was just all worked up. He gets like that sometimes."

"Honestly, Romeo," Julian admitted with a sigh, "I really like you. Like, really, really like you. And I want this to work. But right now, everyone I know hates you."

"And everyone I know hates even the idea of you!" Romeo answered. At Julian's stern look he added, "But I really like you too. And I want this to work."

The two shared a sad sort of smile. "I do too." said Julian. "I could talk to Ty," he offered. "See if he'll meet with you to talk things out."

Romeo nodded again. "I'd like that," he replied, his voice cracking only a little.

As Julian went to grab his phone, he felt a fire growing in his chest. It was no longer the heat of anger but instead a sense of pride. Not in Romeo — though he was glad that Romeo wanted to make things right — but in himself. It turned out, Julian had discovered he could face disaster. The worst could happen, and he didn't have to hide away. There was no way to know how this might go, but he was going to do his best to help. That was something he could offer to the people he loved.

12 Confessions

IT TOOK A WHILE, but as the evening wore on, Julian began to relax into Romeo's company again. As they laced their fingers together, he began to breathe a little deeper.

Romeo told Julian how he'd gotten into it with his parents before he left home that night. Julian breathed with him, running his fingers along Romeo's scar. "I couldn't think of anywhere else to go," Romeo admitted, picking up Julian's hand. "I wish I could make this all go away," he whispered.

"Even me?" Julian teased.

"No," Romeo replied, more serious than Julian expected. "Never you. I never want you to go away."

Julian came closer and they rested against each other. They let time stand still for just a while, softly breathing together.

A knock at the door interrupted their moment. "That must be Sami," Julian said. "I called them before you got here. Can you let them in? I'm gonna call Ty."

Julian left Romeo and Sami alone while he made his call.

"Hey, Jules," Ty answered the phone.

"Hey," Julian replied. Ty was silent, so Julian continued. "I've got kind of a weird request."

"Yeah?" Ty asked.

"You know that guy who hit you? He's . . . at my place."

"Oh, Goddess, Julian, are you all right? Do you need me to come —"

"No, no," Julian interjected, "he . . . he wants to apologize." Julian bit at his nails. "Would you come over and talk with him?"

"I'll see you in a bit," Ty said simply. Before Julian could get another word in, there was a click as Ty ended the call.

Julian's stomach tightened with nerves. "Well, better sooner than later I guess," he mumbled.

"I brought double-chocolate cookies!" called out Sami. Julian grinned — Sami knew those were his favourite.

Romeo was quiet after learning that Ty was on his way. Thankfully, hanging out with Sami was easy, and much more pleasant than nervously counting down the minutes until Ty's arrival.

"Did you see, your mom's protest made the news!" Sami exclaimed. Julian shrugged, reaching for a third cookie to munch. "Your mom's so cool," they raved. "I wish my parents could be like that!" Sami sighed. They looked a bit down for a moment, before perking up again and adding, "Oh! And I heard there's gonna be another big demo on Saturday. But I'm sure you know that. Your mom's probably doing the whole thing!"

Julian just shrugged again. He didn't try to follow all the stuff his mom got up to. Even so, a heavy ball of guilt began to pull Julian down from the inside as he thought of his mother. All the hard work she was doing for her causes, and his friends were getting involved, too. Everyone was doing their part to make the world a better place. What had he ever done for anyone? He'd started following in his mother's footsteps for a while. But now, he wasn't even doing that. The thought of going out there — with all those people, with news cameras and the threats of violence — made his stomach squeeze even tighter.

A burst of laughter from Romeo and Sami broke Julian's train of thought. The pair were cracking up at a joke Julian had missed. He looked at them, smiling a little. Maybe Romeo could fit in with his friends after all. Just then, a knock came at the door, and the three fell silent. Julian's anxiety was already making him feel sick.

Julian let in Ty, and Harvey followed behind. As Julian led the group into the living room, the five of them were quiet as Ty and Harvey sat down together on the old, patched-up loveseat. The rest of the group sat on surrounding chairs of varying types. Sami picked a spot next to Julian. Romeo took a seat on a stool.

Julian glanced at the faces around the room, unsure how this was supposed to play out.

"Romeo," he said at last, "Maybe you can start?" He found his voice again, the one that was steady and direct. Julian stayed focused, willing Romeo to answer.

Romeo took a deep breath. He looked Ty in the eye, and said, "I'm really sorry. For today, for everything. It wasn't funny. It wasn't the kind of guy I want to be."

Julian breathed a short and quiet sigh of relief.

Ty said nothing. He just held Harvey's hand and focused on Romeo.

"I want you to know that I'm . . . I'm gay too," Romeo admitted. "I mean, I think I am anyway. I don't know, but I mean . . . Whatever, the point is, I should have known better. I know it might not make sense, but I didn't want to fight at all."

Julian looked to Ty, but his face was still and impossible to read.

"After I saw you hit Marty, I don't know what came over me," Romeo continued. His voice cracked a little and his face turned red. "Honestly, I'm just really, really sorry. I'll never do something like that again, I swear." After a moment, he added, "Oh, and look . . . My friend who was saying that stuff about the police? I think he was just freaked out, because no one ever calls him on his shit." Ty was stoic as ever while Romeo seemed increasingly flustered. "But, uh, I'm gonna make sure he doesn't call the cops, okay? I promise. I don't want to make things any worse."

The room settled into silence. Everyone was looking from Romeo to Ty and then back to Romeo.

Finally, Ty stood, walked over to Romeo, and extended his hand. "Thanks," he said.

Romeo accepted the hand and Ty pulled him up into a bear hug. Julian's whole body relaxed and he leaned back into the couch. Sami patted his shoulder. When Ty put Romeo back down he said, "You've got some shitty friends though." Romeo nodded and Julian smirked a little.

"I've been pretty shitty myself," Romeo admitted, "until this one appeared in my life." He looked at Julian, giving a hesitant smile.

"He's special like that," Ty replied.

Julian looked away, hiding behind his bangs. He didn't feel special. Guilt still tightened in his gut as he thought about how Ty must have waited for him, how he'd abandoned his cousin when he needed Julian the most.

"When I was away," Ty continued, turning to Julian, "I thought my life was over. But Julian, he wrote to me. He just talked to me, even when everyone else stopped. He kept me going. He just told me about his life, what was going on, and he . . . he reminded me that I had somebody to live for."

Julian looked up, amazed.

"We're family, Jules," Ty said gently. Julian felt

his eyes welling up. "I know we don't have Uncle C around anymore. But I'm always here for you."

Julian leaped up and Ty wrapped him in a big hug. He pressed his tears into his cousin's chest, overflowing in gratitude.

Ty and Harvey decided to stay for dinner. Soon the group was relaxing together, like old friends. After they split a pizza, Julian was cleaning up in the kitchen when Sami joined him. He could hear the other three talking in the next room.

Sami leaned against the door and remarked, "That was pretty brave."

"What, getting pizza with olives *and* pineapple?" Julian laughed, taking apart the pizza box for the recycling.

"You," Sami answered. "You were pretty brave." They shrugged. "Getting those guys together, helping them talk it out."

Julian blushed. "I just wanted them to get along."

A burst of laughter came from the next room over and Julian smiled at the sound.

"Well, good work." Sami grinned.

Eventually, Ty and Harvey headed back home, and Sami caught a ride with them. Julian was left with Romeo, in a house still warm with the energy of their evening.

"Do you want to come up?" Julian offered.

Romeo blushed only a little before following Julian to his room. The pair collapsed onto the bed. Julian began to play with Romeo's hair. Romeo looked up and said, "You've got a pretty amazing life, you know that?"

Julian glanced up and out the window, smiling. He did, didn't he? It hadn't seemed that way before. But today was a good day — good enough that he even had hope for tomorrow.

That was when Julian knew he could finally trust Romeo, and he told him so.

In reply, Romeo showed that he felt the same. "Julian, I love you."

13 Second Chances

JULIAN HUNCHED OVER the kitchen table, attempting to re-write his final paper. He had decided to try again, determined not to fail twice. The topic was written across the top of the outline: "Compare the lives of two of the greatest artists." Julian gritted his teeth, reviewing the readings on Rembrandt, Van Gogh, da Vinci, Picasso, Monet, and Michelangelo. All of them long-dead, European men, none of whom Julian found very inspiring.

With a sigh, Julian's thoughts turned to his new love. Romeo had awoken early and left only a note — he needed to go home and speak with his parents. Julian's stomach clenched with worry and he glanced at his phone. There were no new messages. Turning the device face-down, Julian went back to the computer. He got lost in his thoughts so deeply he didn't even hear Angie come home.

"Hello, my jewel," his mother sang. Julian spun around for a hug. She stepped back, warning, "Careful, these scrubs are filthy!"

As she went to get changed, Julian followed, welcoming the distraction. Angie told him about how long the overnight shift was and the little dramas among the nursing staff. When she sat down, she waved for him to come and rub her shoulders a while. As he did so, she asked, "Whatever happened to that cute snack you brought home?"

Julian was puzzled for a moment, then let out a laugh. "Mom! Romeo wasn't just a snack. I really like him! And he likes me!"

Angie sighed and rolled her eyes before closing them again. She nodded as he found the right spot to work his fingers. "Why don't you go out with someone more on your level?"

"What does that even mean?" Julian asked.

Angie shot him a look. "You know, some of the men — and women — I had when I was in school, they were just like that boy. So I understand! They're pretty and sweet. And you think they can give you the world! But they use you up and toss you out like an orange peel. You need someone who knows how to make marmalade!"

"I don't even know what you're saying," Julian laughed. "Besides, this one, he's different. He said he loves me."

"You met him, what, three days ago?" Angie asked in a salty tone. "They always seem different. Until they all seem the same." She reached up and stroked his hands. "I just worry for you."

"I know," Julian replied. "Actually, I do need some love advice from you. You know Paris?"

"Oh, Goddess!" his mother squealed, spinning around to look at him. "Joanna's girl? Oh, Julian, Paris would be perfect for you!"

"No, Mom!" Julian groaned. "I need your help with how to let her down gently!"

Angie wasn't listening. She was too caught up in going on about Paris, and Paris's mom, and the big political battle against the school board. "Oh, you could go with her to the action on Saturday! Wouldn't that be a cute date! Oh, Jules, why didn't you tell me sooner? Do you think Joanna knows?"

Julian felt himself grow hot. "Mom!" he yelled. "You're not listening! It sounds like me dating Paris would be good for you — not me."

His mother looked stern for just a moment. Julian knew better than to raise his voice to her. But then she seemed to understand and gave him a shrug. "Will you at least try to come on Saturday? I've missed you. You know, when you were just a baby, you came with me to all the protests!"

"You mean you *brought* me to all the protests,"

Julian replied. He sat back down in front of the computer. "I'm not a baby anymore."

Angie kissed the top of his head, saying softly, "Don't I know it. But you'll always be my jewel."

After his mother went off to lie down, Julian was left staring at a blank document, trying to will his essay into existence. He had to get this credit to finish the damn program.

"I thought Classical Art History would be interesting," Julian mumbled to himself. "But this course is the worst." Was all school meant to be like this? Was it ever going to get any easier?

Julian leaned back and wondered about Romeo. What might become of them after graduation? Would Romeo decide to go to university? Or try to get a job? *And*, Julian wondered, *what about me?* School sucked. But maybe it was worth it to see what college could be like. Art school seemed pretty appealing . . .

For the first time in a long time, Julian found he was thinking of his life beyond making it through one day at a time. Putting his head down, he dove into the essay. He wrote down whatever came to mind, resolving to complete it, finish the credit, and get the damn diploma.

The essay was long, hard, and boring. By the time it was almost done, Julian's head was pulsing as he tried to stay focused. He didn't stop until Angie came in, bringing a mason jar of water and a plate of dinner. With a kiss on the forehead, she remarked, "Well, I'm back to it. I'll see you tomorrow."

"You're going back to work already?" Julian asked, looking up at her with distress. "But you just got home!"

"That was hours ago," she told him. She nudged the water in his direction. Julian reluctantly took a sip, only to realize how thirsty he was. He downed the rest in a few gulps. His mom gave him a gentle tap and a kiss on the cheek before ducking out the door.

Julian tried to get back into it, but his focus was gone. Sadness began to creep up, and then quickly crashed over him. Julian fought against the emotional tide as it tried to sweep him away, but he was left feeling numb. It was all he could manage to pull himself upstairs and fall into bed. Once there, he could not guess how long he spent just staring blankly at the ceiling.

Why am I like this? Julian wondered. *Why can't I just get it together?* He sighed as images of his mother came back to him. He saw her walking away, heading back out to another long night after getting so little sleep. Where did she get the energy? How was it possible for her to do so much, when he could barely finish an essay or eat his dinner?

"I'm always letting people down," Julian murmured. He thought of Lyla and her unanswered messages. Of Paris and how he seemed destined to break her heart. Even of Sami. How long until he let them down too? And then there was Ty — sweet Ty. The very thought of him made Julian's stomach roll with guilt.

From the depths of his mind, he pulled up a glimpse of a thin, blurry figure, a flash of red hair, a few distant words. Puzzle pieces of his father, nothing more. "Probably for the best he's not around," mumbled Julian. "I'm sure I'd find a way to disappoint him, too."

Julian let out an ugly cry, shoving his face into the pillow. His body shook as the emotions came back in full force. It felt like he was falling, deeper and deeper. There was no way out, no way things could ever get any better. Finally, as he let go of all hope, a voice came to him.

"We're family, Jules," Ty said in Julian's mind.

Then more voices, swirling together, slowing his fall.

"I miss you," Lyla echoed.

"You're pretty brave," said Sami's voice.

"You'll always be my jewel," his mother added.

"I love you," whispered Romeo.

Julian took a deep breath, and then another. It was painful to come back to his body. His stomach ached and his joints were stiff from sitting still too long. Dragging himself to the bathroom, Julian turned on the shower, and slowly washed it all away.

The water rolled along his arms and down his fingers as he wrapped his arms around himself. Julian cried again but, this time, they were thankful tears. Ty didn't hate him — he had even enjoyed the letters! They had reconnected, and Julian had made it happen! He'd even gotten Ty and Romeo in the same room, talking things out. Sami had been right — that was pretty badass. And if he could make it work with Ty, he knew he could do the same with Lyla. And, maybe, he could even start work on his own issues with himself . . .

"Maybe . . . I don't have to be like Mom," Julian said to himself. "Maybe I can do things in my own way."

Towelling off, Julian was invigorated. He made his way downstairs and finished the dinner Angie had made for him. His eyes moved back to the computer. Writing the essay seemed easier now. One more read-through and he'd send it off.

Finally, with all the drama and hard work over, Julian went back to his paints. He pulled out a canvas, starting out with bursts of red, for love and courage. Streaks of blue, blending into compassionate purple. Sparks of yellow, growing green as they mixed in. Throwing his brush back and forth, Julian laughed as splatter landed against his hands and even up his cheeks. He happily got messy all over again.

14 Surprise

ROMEO'S RETURN was a welcome surprise. Running to the door, Julian jumped into Romeo's arms, covering his cheeks in kisses. But when he pulled away, he could see Romeo wasn't quite as excited. For a moment Julian's stomach did a flip. Was this some sort of break-up house-call? Romeo began to tremble. Flushing red, he backed up to sit down on the porch steps. Julian sat beside him and offered a hand.

"I wish you'd woken me up before you left this morning," Julian began. "I wanted to at least say goodbye." He looked up at the sky as night worked in along its edges. "I was scared that I might never see you again."

Romeo stayed silent, looking away.

"So . . . how did it go?" Julian asked.

Romeo shrugged. "Not so well, with my folks," he admitted. "Or Ben really." He looked down, tracing the scar along his left hand to the base of his golden class ring. "Marty was cool though. You won't believe what he told me, actually." He let out a laugh, but it sounded hollow. Even while he tried to make light of the situation, Romeo's expression was solemn. He started to stumble over his words. His hands were shaking as he burst out, "God, I'm so — I just —"

Julian put his hand over Romeo's, calming him down. The two were quiet together for a while.

"You can cry if you need to," Julian suggested.

Romeo nodded, pulling Julian into an embrace. As they held each other, Julian could hear Romeo's heart beating hard in his chest as he let out a few sobs. Eventually, Romeo stopped shaking and they shared a deep breath. Still holding hands, they pulled a little distance apart. "Maybe we could go for a walk?" Julian offered.

They wandered the neighbourhood, following side streets and exploring empty lots, seeking out places where they could be left alone. The budding greens in the community garden were all asleep and, as the full moon rose above, a few stars winked from the otherwise empty sky. There was a chill in the air, one which brought the couple closer together. They paused to share quick kisses, taking in the quiet secrets of the neighbourhood at night.

Romeo shared how heartbroken he was to have disappointed his family. How scary it was to tell his friends the truth.

"I've just always felt like I was hiding," Romeo said. He looked down at the white flowers budding up along the edges of an empty lot. "But I didn't know why." He sighed. "I just figured that everyone feels that way."

Julian nodded. "A lot of people do." His eyes traced the plants growing through a crack in the concrete and twisting themselves around the remnants of an old chain-link fence. "It's hard to accept the truth about ourselves. Let alone share it with the people you love." He looked back to Romeo with a gentle smile. "I'm proud of you."

Romeo gave a shy grin and replied, "Enough about me. How are you? What did you get up to while I was . . . sharing my truth or whatever?"

Julian shrugged. "I'm fine." Romeo gave him a curious look, waiting for more. Julian smiled and admitted, "Honestly, I'm good. Really good." He looked up and studied the full moon, thinking out loud, "Better than I've felt in a long time." Romeo squeezed his hand. "I started a new painting," Julian went on. "And I finished that essay, so I might get that course credit after all."

"That's awesome!" Romeo exclaimed. Then he asked, in a more sheepish tone, "So . . . what does that mean?"

"Well," Julian grinned, "I'm one step closer to finishing high school." Julian looked at the few stars that made their way through the city lights. "It makes me really think about my life — about my future." He glanced at Romeo and saw him framed by the orange ambience of the night. Julian admitted, "I never really thought I'd have one before . . . before I met you."

Romeo blushed. They shared another kiss before they moved along, deeper into the night.

A breeze brushed past the pair as they approached one of Julian's old hang-outs — the small graveyard, not too far from his home. It was quiet and peaceful, with massive, old trees sheltering the simple gravestones.

"Are you sure?" Romeo asked, looking around nervously.

"People never come in at night," Julian replied. "And," he added with a smile, "you don't need to worry. The ghosts here are harmless. Or, at least, more harmless than most humans." That got a laugh out of Romeo.

They made their way along a worn path, away from the streetlights and into the inviting darkness of the cemetery, lit mainly by the moon above. They were careful not to step on anyone's resting place. A stone angel watched them as they walked by.

Romeo was being oddly silent. Julian spoke up, guessing at his thoughts. "It's gonna work out. With your folks I mean."

"Maybe," Romeo replied.

"Even if they don't come around, I'm here."

"Thanks." After a moment, he added, "I just wish they were more like your mom . . ."

"I guess," Julian said with a shrug. "It can be hard sometimes with her, too," he said. "Sometimes, having a mom who's so busy and so out and so proud, it can get a little lonely. It's easy to feel like I'm just holding her back from all that she could be doing, like, if I could just take care of myself. Or if my dad was around to help. Or if I just . . . wasn't around." Julian nibbled at the edge of his thumbnail.

Romeo held him close. "I don't want you going anywhere."

Julian felt his cheeks go warm. "Thanks." He bit at his nail one more time before adding, "I love you."

"I love you, too," Romeo replied, his voice a hot whisper. "Honestly, all I want is to be with you."

Romeo pulled away from their embrace. In the moonlight, he took Julian's left hand, tenderly kissing the ring finger. Then, getting down on one knee, Romeo pulled off his class ring and offered it to Julian.

Julian's eyes went wide. "I know, not now . . ." Romeo was saying, even as he still held up the ring. "But, one day." Romeo looked up and asked, "Julian Capulet, would you marry me?"

"Oh, Romeo!" Julian exclaimed.

But before he could say another word, a voice called out to them from the darkness.

15 Pulled Back

THREE FIGURES WERE COMING toward the couple. They passed from the streetlights and into the shadows of the graveyard.

"Come on, Romeo, we'd better go," whispered Julian. He pulled at Romeo's sleeve and backed away.

The group's heavy footsteps fell hard against the budding grass, making a squishing noise as they passed over patches of muddy earth. Julian's stomach tensed up and his heart began to race.

"Ben?" Romeo asked. "What are you doing here?"

"You're not so hard to find," the leading stranger grunted. The group was getting close now. Julian could smell the faint but pungent scent of alcohol in the air. Julian could see the one in front, and he immediately recognized his jacket. It was the same kind as Romeo's, embroidered with the fiery basketball and their team name.

Romeo took a step back. Julian began to plan how they could best get past these guys and back to the graveyard entrance. Or maybe they could jump the back fence? His mind ran at double speed, weighing the options, trying to plan a way out of this.

The group called out at Romeo, using names and taunts. Julian looked up in horror as Romeo stopped moving, instead turning to face the group head-on. Was Romeo seriously thinking about fighting these guys? There was no way that was going to work.

Julian's fear spiked when he saw one of the guys was carrying a baseball bat. Vivid memories of his high-school days ran through his mind, and Julian began to tremble. This was it. It was going to be all over. So many times, he'd been so close to taking his own life. Now he'd finally found his will to live and it was going to be stolen from him!

"Come on, guys," Romeo said, trying to reason with them. But the two larger men kept getting closer. The third, who seemed to be their leader, just turned away. "Come on! It's me! How can you —" But before Romeo could finish the thought, Julian saw one of the men gearing up for a hit. That was it. Julian gave Romeo's arm a fierce tug, yanking him away. The couple began to race toward the street. As the men shouted out after them, Julian just hoped Romeo wouldn't be baited again.

Julian's breath was fast and hard, feeling like razors and running his throat raw. With every step, he flitted in and out of real life. He felt himself pulled back into the memories that haunted him.

The pavement is hot and hard against Julian's hands. He hears the skid of car tires. Angry voices call out after him. They're getting ever closer. Julian pushes himself up off the pavement and keeps running. His heartbeat is pounding in his ears.

Julian pumped his legs, trying to stay focused. He and Romeo had to get out of this. He wasn't going to give up now.

There's whispers of gossip all around. Fleeting words hover around like infectious mosquitoes. They spread rumours about him, his absent father, his dyke mother, his hopeless life. Julian hides in a bathroom stall, trying to keep his crying silent.

Romeo was fast, getting a few steps ahead. Julian's chest ached but he kept moving. He had to survive. He had a reason to live. He had people who loved him. He had more still to do. He wasn't going to give in to the fear.

His mother's face is full of pity as she brings him dinner in bed. Julian has no appetite. He sees the long days and nights passing in a blur. He floats in the numbness of isolation. He stares at a half-finished letter to Ty, filled with promises he knows he can't keep. Somewhere, his phone is ringing, but he is not going to answer.

Romeo reached back for him and Julian tried to grasp his hand. If only he could just reach him, Julian knew they would be safe. They would get out of this. He would wake up tomorrow and this would have been little more than a bad dream. But, before they could reach one another, Julian felt a yank from behind. Then there was a hard push against his back, and a dizzying pain as he fell to the ground. And then he knew nothing for a while.

When Julian regained his senses, he heard the sounds of a struggle. There was a thud and Julian caught a glimpse of Romeo colliding with one of the men as he tackled him to the ground. He rolled over to see Romeo thrown back, hitting one of the gravestones. The two men fell onto him with punches and kicks. That was when Julian spied the bat, sitting nearby in the grass.

Grabbing the weapon, Julian ran at the attackers. He didn't allow himself a second to reconsider. He was not going to run away from this, not when Romeo needed him. A fire was building up inside him, starting in his stomach and rolling out through his entire body. Bounding forward, Julian remembered all the bigots at school, all the hate he'd endured, every dirty look and cruel word. He swung at the men attacking Romeo with every bit of his pent-up rage.

Before he could land a single blow, a fist slammed into Julian's gut. The wind was knocked out of him. Julian gasped and keeled over, clutching his torso. "Faggot," one of the men spat out. The word shook in the air. Julian looked over at Romeo, who was limp against a gravestone and looking pale. The two men turned back to work him over.

Dizziness filled Julian's head as he tried to stand. He couldn't find the strength to get up. His stomach was tight and its sick feeling ran up into his lungs, forcing a painful coughing fit. Prickles of dirt and grass scratched against his skin. Again, he tried to move himself from the ground. But every breath in was a losing battle. The world had begun to spin.

"Romeo, please don't be dead," Julian managed to murmur. He watched, helplessly, as Romeo was tossed back and forth between the attackers. This was it, Julian realized, this was the end. He could hear the squelch of boots against the wet mud and the thud of their impact with Romeo's limp body. Losing his grip on reality, Julian began to slip out of consciousness. He only wished he could be a little closer to Romeo. He wanted to reach out and hold his hand. He didn't want to go into this darkness alone.

16 Coming To

JULIAN SPUN IN A WORLD of nothing, and it was oddly noisy. His thoughts were wordless, pure colour, movement, vibration. Then, as if waking from a dream, he felt himself pulled back toward something familiar.

There was a heavy weight on top of his chest. It was hard to open his eyes. But there were the loud noises again, clearer now. Words began to come to him, as if from a distance or from the other side of thick glass. He was back inside his body, aching and stiff, like he'd slept in a strange position. Julian managed to push his eyes open. Above him were bright lights and a bland, beige ceiling. Looking around, he saw blue curtains, a matching bedspread, and clear tubes running in and out of him.

The memory of what happened rushed back with a vengeance.

In his mind's eye, Julian felt himself return to that hard ground, damp with blood. He was surrounded by the smell of the dirty leaves, itching grass, the grunting of his attackers. He remembered trying to fight back, and getting a blow to his stomach. There was that sharp and sudden pain. He remembered falling, losing his breath, and being barely able to move. Everything after that was misty and faint. How had they survived? His mind rec a vague sound, maybe an ambulance. And there had been strange voices too, asking him questions. He couldn't remember the details of what had been said. He opened his eyes again and stared up at the fluorescent lights.

Julian wiggled his fingers and toes. Everything

seemed to be responding as usual. He kept wiggling, not wanting to risk slipping back into that cold memory. As he focused on his hands and feet, a familiar voice boomed into the room. "My baby!" Before he could look, he was wrapped in his mother's arms. Her warmth and familiar smell enveloped him.

Julian felt a pang of guilt. She must have been so worried. He was already racking up the ways in which this could be his fault.

"Oh, my precious jewel!" Angie sobbed into his hair. She kissed his forehead over and over. "You're awake! Thank the Goddess!"

Julian squirmed, overwhelmed by her affection, even as he was glad to have her close.

Angie recounted the story of Julian's arrival at the hospital. "As soon as you and that Romeo boy got here, they realized who you were," she told him. "And I had to go off shift! I had to just sit there in the waiting room." She scowled, her arms crossed in frustration.

Julian breathed a sigh of relief. Romeo was safe

too. Or, at least, not left behind in the cemetery mud.

"And you'll never guess who I met there," his mother went on. Julian raised a brow in response, not having much energy for conversation. "A woman calling herself Mrs. Maria Montague." Seeing his surprised expression, Angie nodded with satisfaction. "Yes! Apparently, she was the one that called it in. She saw the attack!"

Julian was shocked. Romeo's mother had been there? That sounded like something he would have remembered.

"She told me she had been tracking Romeo's cell phone," Angie explained. "We had a while in there to talk." Angie shrugged and said in a loud whisper, "She does seem to be an odd woman."

Romeo had told him that his mother was overbearing, anxious, and often distant. Maybe that's what Angie meant? Julian couldn't stop himself from fixating on the fact that she'd been tracking Romeo's phone. It was an uncomfortable thought, even if it turned out to be helpful at the end of the day. His mind was buzzing with questions. Julian only partially listened to all his mother had to say as she recounted her overnight struggle with the hospital, Mrs. Montague, and her own worries about her son.

Eventually, Julian found the strength to speak. "Where's Romeo?" His lips cracked as they parted over the name.

Angie gave Julian a peeved look, and he managed to return the expression. Yes, it was understandable she was upset. But she wasn't the one who had been beaten within an inch of her life!

With a sigh, she stood up to pull back the blue curtain surrounding Julian's bed. There, sleeping soundly, was Julian's love. Romeo looked peaceful like that, curled up in the adjacent hospital bed. But a turn of his head showed that his face had been stamped red and purple, and much of his upper body was bandaged. As if on cue, his eyes fluttered open. He winced as a smile rolled across his battered face.

"You're alive," Julian croaked. His eyes welled up with tears.

"I promised . . . I wouldn't leave you," Romeo croaked back.

"Teenagers, so dramatic," Angie teased, a tear still in her eye. Julian shot her a look and she winked at him, leaning down to wrap him in another hug. Then she made her way over to Romeo, fussing over him and offering ice chips. Seeing Angie in full-on momma mode, Julian relaxed a little. He and Romeo were in safe hands with her around.

It wasn't until he heard a new voice that Julian noticed there was someone else in the room — Romeo's mother. She barely acknowledged the presence of Julian or Angie, focusing exclusively on Romeo. She said something to her son, too quiet for the others to hear. The tension of the room went up a few notches as Julian and Angie both looked from Romeo's mother to one another, exchanging looks of concern.

Romeo fell asleep again quickly and Mrs. Montague left shortly after. "Blessed be," mumbled Julian under his breath.

By the time visiting hours rolled around, Angie had already fetched snacks, magazines, flowers, and stuffed animals from the hospital gift shop. She placed them around the room with serious consideration. Julian didn't mind. He knew his mother would never be satisfied just sitting around and waiting for him to get better. Plus, it was nice to have her caregiving energy flowing freely without focusing solely on him.

That day, Julian and Romeo had their first proper visitor — one of Romeo's friends who called himself Marty. He came in with his head hanging like a sorrowful pup, looking positively pitiful. He wore that same sports jacket, with the blazing basketball. Julian shivered a little at the sight.

After Marty and Romeo shared a quiet conversation, Marty came over to meet Julian. He offered him a card. Julian was surprised to find it was signed from Guyna!

"Yeah, Romeo and I ran into her at that diner she works at," Marty explained, letting out a nervous laugh. "I guess we had actually met before that — at that party. She — er, he," Marty shrugged, "freaked me out so much that night, hardcore flirting with me!"

"Sounds about right," Julian chuckled.

Marty seemed to brighten up a little, and even blushed slightly. "Anyway, we were . . . together last night. When we got the news, I mean, about you two." Marty looked down again, studying his shoes.

Julian just nodded, curious but too tired to ask Marty for details. He was sure Guyna would fill him in later.

"She's stuck at work," Marty explained. "But she picked the card for you."

Julian looked down at the cover of the card. It featured a naked man standing at a mountain's peak. The caption read, *You Made It!* Inside was simply the letter 'G' next to a lipstick kiss with a goatee outlined in eyeliner. Julian smirked.

Romeo had drifted off again before Marty even left. He slept most of that day and into the night.

Julian began to worry, but Angie assured him it was perfectly normal. "His body's trying to heal," she told Julian, softly petting his hair. "Plus, he's full to the brim with pain meds." She kissed Julian's forehead. "Just let him rest."

Julian still worried. He fidgeted with his fingernails. He wasn't sleeping as much as Romeo. Did that mean that his body wasn't healing? Or did it mean that Romeo was much worse off? As Julian tried to rest, his dreams were haunted with memories of that fateful night. The faces of their attackers morphed into those of his high-school bullies. He woke up in a cold sweat, calling out for Romeo. Angie rushed to his side, groggily trying to reassure him. He was safe now.

17

A Call to Action

LYLA AND ROSE WERE the first to arrive on Julian and Romeo's second day in the hospital. The girls brought treats and get-well-soon gifts. The room was starting to look like a second gift shop!

Rose rushed to Romeo's side, while Lyla came to see Julian, offering chocolate.

"How you holding up?" she asked.

Julian took a chocolate and chewed on it. He looked Lyla over. "Not great," he admitted.

Lyla wrinkled her eyebrows. "It's not your fault."

"You don't know that," Julian replied, pulling back. "I could have . . . I should have . . ." He felt his face grow hot and sighed in frustration.

"You're still alive. That's something, right?" said Lyla. "You survived. That's incredible."

Julian looked over at Romeo. He *was* thankful they were alive. Angie was catching a quick nap in the visitor's chair, and Julian's chest squeezed a little at the thought of how she would feel if he wasn't around anymore. He could see that Lyla was glad he was alive, too. Finally, he looked down at his own body. As bruised and sore as he was, Julian remembered the last moment before he blacked out. He remembered how scared he'd been that this could be the end. Maybe surviving was pretty good, given what could have been.

"I guess," Julian finally answered.

"You're more than the hate people put on you, you know," Lyla said in a gentle voice.

Julian just nodded and looked away.

Lyla placed the rest of the gifts they brought on

the windowsill. There were some balloons, a stuffed animal, and more snacks. "What's this?" she asked, picking up something small that glinted in the light. Julian recognized it instantly — Romeo's class ring! His mind suddenly raced to remember everything that had happened before the attack.

Julian reached for the ring and smiled up at Lyla. "It's Romeo's." It was too big for his finger, but Julian slipped it on anyway.

Lyla glanced to where Romeo was chatting with Rose. "You know, they're best friends, too?" She chuckled. "What are the chances?"

"Yeah?" Julian blushed and looked down. "Am I . . . still your best friend?"

Lyla looked surprised. "Of course!" she answered.

"It's just . . ." Julian said, "Here I am. Helpless. Again! And my mom, and you, have to take care of me — again!" He sighed. "I told myself I wouldn't do that to you."

"Julian," said Lyla, her voice more stern than he had expected, "You've always been there for me. So I'm always going to be there for you." Her face softened as she added, "You're more than the expectations people put on you, too, you know. You can just be you."

Julian looked down. "Thanks," he mumbled. "But . . ." his voice trailed off. "I mean, we've barely talked in a year!"

Lyla shrugged. "You were going through a hard time." She looked over at her girlfriend. "And I've been . . . busy." Julian followed her gaze. They watched Romeo and Rose, laughing together and hugging. "I'm sorry," Lyla said at last. Julian gave her a quizzical look. "I should have made more of an effort," she admitted. "When you stopped answering, I should have shown up in person. Or tried to talk to your mom. But then I met Rose, and everything changed." She gently sighed, gazing at her partner.

Julian took Lyla's hand. "I'm sorry, too. And I get it — falling in love can really turn everything upside down! Look at us, turning into a couple of sappy romantics!"

Lyla laughed and passed him another chocolate.

With each bite, Julian was feeling better.

As Rose and Lyla were getting ready to leave, a familiar and unwelcome figure appeared in the doorframe. Mrs. Montague was back again. She stood quietly just outside the room, looking hesitant.

"Hi there," Angie spoke up, fully awake from her afternoon nap.

Mrs. Montague gave a quick glance out of the corner of her eye and a cursory nod toward Angie.

"We were just going," Rose said, tugging on Lyla. "We'll see you around."

The two young women waved goodbye and were out the door in a flash, leaving Julian and Angie alone with Mrs. Montague. Romeo had drifted off while talking to Rose and slept on soundly.

Mrs. Montague simply walked over to Romeo and put her hand on his head. She began what looked like a quiet prayer. Julian watched for a while but he began to feel like he was the one invading her space. So, he looked away and went back to studying Romeo's class ring.

After a while, Romeo awoke, but Mrs. Montague

did not become any more talkative. It seemed like she was waiting for her son to apologize. The concept might have made Julian laugh if he wasn't so angry with the woman. If anyone was to blame for this, Julian decided, it was Mrs. Montague and her husband. They were the ones who made Romeo run off in the first place. They were the kind of people who tried to pass their bigotry down to their children, by force if necessary, all under the guise of protecting them. Julian could tell that Angie was thinking something similar, and they shared a disapproving look.

Before the mothers and their sons could interact, a new pair of visitors arrived. First, a teacher from Romeo's school burst into the room, desperately apologetic. He was followed by a woman who walked in as if she held all the solutions. Julian recognized her right away. He'd most recently seen her marching down Osborne Street. It was Joanna Duke, Paris's mother and the big-time activist who had been organizing with Angie.

"Mrs. Duke?" Romeo said. "What are you doing here?"

"You know her, too?" Julian asked.

"She's the vice principal at my school," Romeo replied. "Wait — how do you know her?"

"Don't you watch the news?" Angie asked.

Joanna Duke began speaking over all of them. "Please know I am sincerely sorry for what has happened. The offending parties have been apprehended, or shall be shortly."

Julian wasn't sure how he felt about that statement — or this woman, for that matter. She spoke like someone about to ask for a political favour.

"Romeo, please be advised that your suspension has been lifted. Clearly, we misunderstood the situation."

Romeo nodded. "Uh, thanks."

"Mrs. Montague," Joanna Duke said with a nod, then turned to Julian's mother. "Angie. Would you both join me in the hall? I have something I'd like to discuss."

"If it's about us, just say it to us!" Julian interjected.

"I'm not so sure that's a good idea," Joanna Duke began.

Julian was about to argue, but when he turned to

his partner for support, he saw that Romeo was already slipping back into sleep. Maybe she had a point. Romeo probably had already had enough talk for one day.

"Well, I'm coming anyway," Julian said. He got up from the bed, a little shaky. Feeling awkward in his hospital gown, he made his way to the hall, following the three women.

Joanna Duke began, addressing the two mothers. "There is clearly a great need to address the homophobia and transphobia that remains persistent in our educational system." Julian nodded. He agreed with her on that at least. "To this end, I have been leading a group demanding that the board require all public schools to include a course on gender and sexuality studies."

"No shit, Sherlock," Angie replied, hand on her hip. "Half the meetings have been held at my house!" Mrs. Montague seemed to curl back a little at Angie's language. Julian smirked.

Joanna Duke gave a quick nod. "Of course. So, as some of you may know, this course would aim to empower students to understand themselves, dispel ignorance, and prevent the kind of hateful actions these boys suffered just a day ago."

"All right," Mrs. Montague said. Her voice was surprisingly calm, yet still cautious. "What does that mean for us? And my Romeo?"

Joanna Duke nodded again. "My request, for you both, is to allow your sons to share their story. Allow them to speak at the rally next week."

Angie's whole face lit up with excitement. But she held her tongue, saying simply, "It depends on what Julian wants."

"I don't think that is a good idea," Mrs. Montague replied. "It's just, with all that's happened, is it wise to expose them to more . . . attention?"

Julian felt himself choke up for a moment. He realized that he actually agreed with Mrs. Montague. For that very reason, though, he began to question his first thoughts. He looked to his mother, who simply raised her eyebrow. Turning back, he looked at Romeo through the window. He was sound asleep.

"Let me ask him," Julian suggested.

18 *Choice*

"YOU'RE GOING HOME," said the afternoon nurse to Julian. She seemed to be in her mid-fifties, with short, brown hair, and a clinical, direct tone.

Julian's stomach clenched up. "What, really?" he asked. He turned to Romeo. "What about him?"

The nurse looked down at his chart. "Let's see, it looks like you've had a few stitches, and definite bruising. But otherwise you seem to be in perfectly good health." She let the paper fall back against the clipboard. She said again, almost mechanically, "After forty-eight hours of supervision, the doctors have concluded you're well enough to go home and rest." She passed him a prescription slip. "If you're still in pain, you can take two of these at a time. Just speak with the pharmacist on your way out."

"But what about Romeo?" Julian asked again, perturbed.

The nurse huffed and replied, "I don't have orders for him. Just you."

Julian's heart sank. He looked to his mother, hoping she might intervene. But Angie just nodded her head. "Julian, he's got a broken rib and internal damage," She kissed Julian's forehead. "Your stitches will heal quickly, my jewel. Romeo will need more time."

"If you want to stay," said the nurse, "you'll need to do it in the waiting room, like everyone else. We've got more people coming in. We need this bed open."

Agonized that they were going to be apart, Julian went to his partner's side. Romeo was awake, and held

Julian's hand, smiling softly. "Go ahead," Romeo said. "I'll be out in a day or two, you'll see."

Reluctantly, Julian agreed. He certainly didn't mind the idea of sleeping in his own bed again. They shared a quick kiss and Julian was on his way.

Julian and Angie took a taxi home. Halfway there, Julian looked up at his mother to ask, "Wait, what day is it?"

"It's Friday, Jules," Angie replied. Julian's stomach immediately squeezed itself into a knot. "Something wrong?" she asked, looking Julian over as he nervously nibbled at his nails.

Julian shook his head, not saying anything. Instead, he pulled out his cell and fired off a text to Paris. He asked if they could meet up and just talk. He didn't have the energy to go out for dinner, but didn't want to host her at his house. He asked her to wait for him at the community garden. She agreed, emojis bookending her texts.

Julian's stomach got tighter as the cab got closer to home. Angie brought him inside, wrapped him up in bed, and left him water. Then she promptly went back out to a planning meeting for Saturday's big protest. Once he'd heard the door shut, Julian popped a painkiller, threw on a comfortable outfit, and made his way to the door.

Outside, the street was chilly, like it had been on that fateful night just a few days ago. Julian felt his fear mounting as he tried to pass through the small broken gate that marked the edge of their yard. The shadows played tricks on him, looking like people out of the corner of his eye. His heart began to beat fiercely. This was a mistake. He couldn't do this. Julian ran back inside, slamming the door and sliding the lock shut. Paris was probably already on her way to the garden, or even there waiting for him. He couldn't cancel now. Pulling out his cell, he decided to call for backup.

"Sami, it's me," Julian began.

There was a shriek on the line and he had to pull the phone back from his ear. Sami began to gush about how scared they'd been, how sorry they were that they hadn't been able to visit the hospital, and they quickly fell into a diatribe about what a week it had been.

"It's fine, it's fine," Julian said quickly. "Are you free right now? I need you to come over here as fast as you can."

Within minutes, Sami was at the door. "What do you need?" they asked, breathing heavily.

"Did you run here?" asked Julian.

"Biked," Sami replied. They gestured to a rusty pink bicycle locked to the fence out front.

"I . . . can't leave the house," Julian admitted, looking at his feet.

"Why do you have to leave?"

"Paris is waiting for me."

Sami reached out, offering their arm as support. "I can walk with you, if you want."

Julian took Sami's arm. He felt silly, but thankful. "I'm sorry," he said.

"You've got nothing to be sorry for," Sami replied. "I think this is pretty brave."

"I don't feel very brave," Julian whimpered. He

reached in his pocket and squeezed Romeo's ring. It gave him the strength to take a deep breath and step outside again.

"What are you gonna say to her?" Sami asked once they were a few steps from the house.

"I don't know," he admitted.

Paris was waiting at the entrance to the garden. Her hair was in a long braid down her back and her makeup made her bright eyes look larger than life. When she saw Julian on Sami's arm, she gave a curious look.

"Sami, can you maybe . . . leave us alone for a minute?" Julian asked.

"No problem," replied Sami. They walked toward the edge of the lot and stood a bit awkwardly, trying not to eavesdrop.

Julian took Paris into the garden. He studied the little buds that were fighting their way up from the dirt. She looked at him expectantly.

"About the date," Julian began, searching for his words.

"Are you hurt?" Paris asked, looking at his bruises. "Do you need to reschedule?"

"I . . . I need to cancel," he admitted.

"Oh." Paris looked down at the ground.

"I'm sorry, Paris, honestly." The two stood in silence for a while. "You deserve someone who is so excited to be with you."

Paris just shrugged.

The night was oddly quiet. The streetlights behind them made her brilliant eyes sparkle as they welled up with tears. "Why can't *you* be excited to be with me?" she asked.

Julian didn't know what to say, so he looked away. His gaze moved up into the sky and studied the waning moon.

"I like you, so much," she confessed. "And I–I just wanted one chance, to see if maybe you could like me, too."

Julian forced himself to look her in the eye. He had to tell the truth. "Paris, I'm really sorry. I just don't feel that way for you."

"Then why did you say yes?!" she demanded.

Julian winced. "It was . . . a mistake," he admitted. "I met someone else and he . . . he made me realize what it means to really want to be with someone." He tried to take her hand. "Honestly, you're amazing, it's just —"

Paris pulled away. "I'm so sick of being everyone's second choice!"

Julian was winded, more from surprise than anything else. He felt himself begin to shake. Sami stepped forward, rushing towards them.

"What do you want?" Paris asked sharply.

Sami offered an arm to Julian before turning back to Paris. "I'm just here to take care of Julian," they said calmly.

"Oh," moaned Paris. "I just . . ." She sighed. "This just sucks."

Julian nodded in agreement.

"Do you wanna talk about it?" Sami asked Paris. "Julian needs to go home and rest. But how about you and me go grab something to eat?"

Paris nodded. She wiped her tears, smudging her makeup. "I'd like that."

The pair walked Julian home in relative silence. But it was less uncomfortable than he'd feared. Paris even offered him a gentle hug before she left. Taking Sami's arm, she walked down the street, toward the bright lights of the main road.

Julian went inside, thankful to be alone again. He clutched Romeo's ring as he curled up in bed.

19 Only the Beginning

THE GOLDEN STATUE ATOP the legislature building glittered in the bright day. Below, a crowd chanted, "Two, four, six, eight! Schools are made to educate!"

It was a larger turnout than Julian had expected. People of all ages turned out with signs that read things like, *We DO need some Education! Teach the kids on Liberation!* and *Bullies Beware, the Queers are Here!*

Julian shuffled his feet, waiting on the edge of the crowd for Romeo to arrive. His stomach turned with anxiety. He could see Angie, sporting a bright pink shirt and handing out buttons and flyers. "Wanna help?" she called out to him. Julian shook his head and politely refused. Finally, a familiar truck rolled up and Julian ran over to meet it.

Ty came out first, giving Julian a wave before going to the back of the truck to grab the fold-out wheelchair for Romeo. Harvey came second, going to the passenger side where Romeo sat and offered him a hand.

"You're really here!" Julian gasped.

"And so are you!" Romeo replied with a grin.

"Little Jules," Ty smiled. "All grown up and ready for his first real rally." He opened up his arms. "How does it feel?"

Julian jumped for a big bear hug from Ty. "Scary! Loud! Exciting!" he answered.

Ty laughed. "Sounds about right. We brought you something," he said, motioning to Harvey.

"Oh?" Julian asked, turning his head.

Harvey passed him a small, palm-sized bag, giving

a gentle smile and a nod.

"I gave it to Harvey when we started going out. But we agree, you should have it," Ty explained. "It's from Uncle C."

"Your dad?" Romeo asked.

Julian nodded. "He gave you a bag?"

"It's what's inside the bag, silly," Ty teased.

Julian pulled the string on the soft pouch and reached inside. He felt something small, cold, and metallic. He pulled out a palm-sized pendant on a silver chain. Engraved in the pendant was a deer with a word above it, *Amo*. The medallion looked positively ancient.

"It's from our family," Ty explained. "It's our family's crest, more or less. The word means 'I love.' And that's our animal too — the stag."

Julian's eyes welled up as he thought back to his distant memories of his father. "Little fawn," he said aloud.

"Yeah, that's what he used to call you." Ty smiled. "He loved you a lot, you know."

Ty moved to help Julian put on the necklace. Then Julian took Romeo's ring from his pocket. "Here," he said, "I want to wear this one, too." The ring slid down the silver chain and rested, next to the medallion, close to Julian's heart.

"Take care of yourself," Ty said, hugging Julian again. "You too," he added over Julian's shoulder, speaking to Romeo.

"You're not staying?" Julian asked.

Ty and Harvey shared a look. "Just give us a call. We can pick you both up when you're done," said Ty. Harvey gave a nod in agreement. The couple then clambered back into their truck and drove away, leaving Romeo and Julian alone with the growing crowd.

Julian moved alongside Romeo slowly, helping with the chair when asked. They worked their way along the edge of the crowd. Angie came back into view, waving widely and throwing out rainbow lanyards. Joanna Duke was alongside her, looking serious.

Angie ran over, embracing Julian and kissing his head. "How is my darling jewel?" She pulled back to look him in the eye. "Are you sure you're up for this? How are you feeling? Are you tired? Do you need anything?"

Julian laughed. "Mom, I'm all right, really."

Angie gave a soft smile, then turned her gaze to Romeo. "And what about you?"

Romeo blushed and gave a quiet nod. "I'll live," he replied.

"Thank the Goddess for that," Angie murmured.

From farther away, Joanna Duke waved them over. "Come to the front of the rally when you're ready."

Julian clenched up and gave a nod in return.

Romeo seemed to sense his anxiety. He looked up at Julian and asked, "What are you thinking?"

"Maybe this was a mistake," Julian replied.

"Do you want to leave?" asked Romeo.

Julian's hands moved to the precious pendants around his neck, and he took a breath. Looking into Romeo's eyes, he answered, "If you can do this, I can do this." With a sigh, he added, "I just wish you didn't have to go back to the hospital."

Romeo nodded. "I don't like it either . . ." He took Julian's hand. "But we've got the rest of our lives together to look forward to."

For a while, the couple just watched the crowd go by. Julian caught sight of Paris, with Sami at her side, and the two had their hair styled into matching colourful ponytails. They waved at Julian with big smiles. Then Romeo motioned at another pair of familiar faces — there was Guy, sporting a black tuxedo-style T-shirt, joined by a figure in a masquerade mask and a long summer dress. "I think that's Marty!" Romeo exclaimed.

"They look stunning together." Julian grinned.

Even Lyla and Rose made it out. They were carrying a large sign together and shouting confidently with the crowd. When they saw Romeo and Julian they came running over. After giving him a careful hug, Lyla put a hand on Julian's shoulder and told him, "You got this," before vanishing with Rose into the crowd.

"Are you ready?" Romeo asked.

"As I'll ever be," Julian replied.

Julian's stomach still had butterflies as they went up the ramp, onto the stage. He heard the cameras begin to click with excitement. Joanna Duke stood off to the side, watching everything. Her expression, Julian decided, was one of stoic respect.

"Um, hi," Julian said into the microphone. His voice bounced out of the speakers on either side. The crowd continued to mill about, with only a few people turning their heads. Julian saw Angie was already crying.

He turned to Romeo. "Did you . . . prepare anything?"

Romeo shrugged. "Not really. You?"

Julian shrugged back. "Well, one of us should say something, right?"

Romeo nodded. "Go for it."

Julian spoke up again. "Hello, everyone. I'm Julian Capulet. And this is Romeo Montague. We're here to today to . . . talk to you."

There were a few smiles, more turning heads. The crowd began to simmer down. Julian took a deep breath, closed his eyes, and pictured a blank canvas. He was going to paint it with everything he had inside of him. All that anger, fear, sadness, guilt — and maybe even pride, and joy, and hope.

"I was queer before I was even born," he began. A few people laughed. "And my best friend, she had her first kiss with a girl before we were ten!" More laughter. "I never had to be ashamed of who I am. Not until I was made to feel that way. They called me names, they chased me home, they even told me to kill myself. And . . . I almost did." The words seemed to echo endlessly. Romeo squeezed his hand and Julian pressed forward. "But I don't want to die. I want to live. I want all of us to live!"

The crowd began to cheer. A rush went through Julian's whole body. He didn't dare open his eyes as he went on. "Last week, Romeo and I were attacked. It was . . . almost the end." The crowd was silent, hanging on his every word. "Now, I don't know if this cause we're fighting for is going to be the solution. I don't know if it's going to untangle all that messy, complicated, hurtful, and hateful stuff that gets put on us. But I know this."

Julian took another deep breath. "We are alive for a purpose — to love each other. To love ourselves, as we are. And if this has even a chance of helping us do that, well, I think it's something worth fighting for." Julian paused. The silence was intense. He began to feel dizzy. Squeezing Romeo's hand, he finished by saying, "Don't you?"

The crowd screamed with excitement. Julian opened his eyes in surprise. It was bright and there was noise all around — snapping cameras, chants and shouts, and, somewhere, a voice saying his name. "Julian . . . Julian . . ."

It was Romeo. "Julian," Romeo said again, smiling. "That was amazing."

Julian nodded and quietly replied, "Let's get out of here."

They made their way off the stage and managed to hide away from the crowd, under the shade of a large oak tree.

"Wow." Romeo looked at Julian in awe.

Julian just nodded and took a few deep breaths. That had been, by far, the most frightening thing in the last couple of weeks.

After a moment, Romeo asked, "So what now?"

Julian gently smiled, unsure if Romeo meant this moment, or the rest of their lives. But it didn't matter. Leaning down, he answered with a kiss. Julian felt the ring and the amulet around his neck gently chime as they touched. Holding on to a piece of his past and a piece of his future, Julian knew, this was only the beginning.

Acknowledgements

So many people made this book possible — including you, the reader! Thanks so much for helping this story come to life!

I'd like to give special appreciation to Shane Camastro, for supporting the stories of Romeo & Julian, even when they were still just daydreams.

A big hug for Kat Mototsune — thank you for editing this text. Your support, guidance, and kindness were all essential for my writing process.

Thank you to Louis Esmé. Your feedback on this story was essential. I will forever be thankful for both your honesty and friendship.

Bridget Liang, your collaboration and comradeship made writing so much richer! I know you will continue to make amazing things.

Much love to all the Phoenix Nest — past, present, and future! Thank you for taking care of each other, laughing together, and living out all that real love can be.

Thanks to all my holos back in the day in Winnipeg. You were the best friends a messed up teen like me could ever ask for. And special shout out to Ariyanna — you'll always be my big sister.

Thank you, Iris Robin, for all your comments, questions, ideas, and enthusiasm! You're a truly fabulous friend.

Many thanks to Kate Welsh, your brainstorming sessions and helpful ideas are all over this work.

Sienna Rachelle — many thanks to you, and all your family, for being absolutely weird and wonderful.

All my love to Andrew McAllister — your companionship means the world to me. And to Hannah Dees — I can't wait for us to start our family together.

Finally, Bill & Cheryl Telford, Tony Harwood-Jones, and Heather Dixon. You have both literally and figuratively made me who I am today. Thank you for everything.